SYSTEMA PARADOXA

ACCOUNTS OF CRYPTOZOOLOGICAL IMPORT

VOLUME 14

OUT FOR BLOOD

A TALE OF THE ROUGAROU

AS ACCOUNTED BY JORIE RAO

NEOPARADOXA

Pennsville, NJ

2023

PUBLISHED BY
NeoParadoxa
A division of eSpec Books
PO Box 242
Pennsville, NJ 08070
www.especbooks.com

ISBN: 978-1-956463-15-6
ISBN (ebook): 978-1-956463-14-9

Interior Design: Danielle McPhail
www.sidhenadaire.com

Cover Art: Jason Whitley
Cover Design: Mike and Danielle McPhail, McP Digital Graphics
Interior Illustration: Jason Whitley

Copyediting: Greg Schauer and John L. French

Dedication

DAD—
I WROTE US THE RECONCILIATION WE NEVER GOT.
THERE'S MONSTERS IN THIS VERSION,
BUT IT STILL COUNTS.

CHAPTER ONE

"We need to get our stories straight, Prudence." Dad gripped his cell phone in his clean hand as he talked to me.

The entire room looked unreasonably clean. Except for the splintered front door, the smashed vase, and, of course, the blood-stained floor—mine from the cuts on my hands and Mom's from when the beast ripped into her neck—everything else remained intact, looking for all the world like a tragedy hadn't occurred.

Nothing made sense. Not Dad's insistence on syncing up our stories, not my untainted clothes, Mom's shredded, blood-soaked ones, or Dad's Motley Crue shirt and jeans stained from when he cradled Mom's body.

"Prudence, listen. It was a wolf that got in, okay? A *wolf*." Dad's voice trembled, but hard lines etched the corners of his ice-blue eyes as his lips pulled into a severe frown. "Kid, it's okay. You're okay."

"How can you even *say* that?"

He withdrew, eyes flaring, and looked over his shoulder to where Mom lay. "I shouldn't have. I'm sorry."

I nodded. It wasn't enough, but I didn't tell him that.

"I know what happened calls for an explanation, and I promise you'll get one, but before that, I need you to tell the cops you saw a wolf. It's the only story they'll understand."

"It *was* a wolf," I told him. Albeit one that stood on two legs, towering and ravenous, *but* it had a snout and fur and sharp canines and claws at the ends of its fingers and toes.

"Yes, exactly." Dad put his clean hand on my shoulder the way he used to when I got an answer to one of his pop quizzes right.

I shrugged away from his touch.

If he noticed, he ignored it, crossing the living room to pull the storm door closed as he called 911. "Hello, yes, my wife's been attacked." He placed the shotgun he'd used to chase the beast off in the crook of his elbow. "Yes, by an animal. I took a shot at it, but it got away." A long pause stretched, during which Dad looked at Mom. Finally, he said, "No, she—she's dead."

After hanging up, he retrieved the broom and dustpan from the kitchen and brushed the wooden fragments away from the front door. The wolf-man had forced its hand through, shooting the doorknob out, splintering the wooden frame.

And I'd just stood there. Screaming.

"Mom." I choked on the word.

"Prue, deep breaths," Dad said.

I tried, but panic assailed me. My shoulders slumped. I forced myself to look at her—brown eyes, open and expressionless. My chest heaved, and I went limp. Crashing to the floor, I dragged myself over to her rigid form.

I whispered to her, "I'm sorry."

A succession of new noises disturbed the unnatural silence as the cops and EMTs arrived.

This can't be real… The thought resounded in my mind as more people arrived. Eventually, my sister, Justice, walked through the front door accompanied by the uniformed cop who'd been sent to get her from her friend's house.

The sight of her made my throat feel thick. I took a deep, pained breath. Her chestnut hair was tied in a messy bun with one of Mom's spare scrunchies. A yellow velvet one. She had her backpack hooked over one shoulder, half-zipped, with clothes sticking out. She hadn't changed out of her green flannel pajama bottoms and oversized *Star Wars* shirt. Her feet were bare.

I hugged myself and leaned against the door frame, not trusting my legs to hold me.

I watched her chin quiver. Then she was crying and moving toward me. Her bare feet slapped against the hardwood floor. She sidestepped debris, her eyes fixed on mine, as she moved past the EMT loading Mom's limp form into a body bag.

How could I have let this happen? How could I have let Justice down like this?

She pulled me toward her, and when I resisted, she didn't say anything, just pulled me harder until we collapsed into one another like two demolished buildings. We crumpled to the floor as one, curling against the door frame, both shaking with our sobs.

Instantly, every noise became too much. My sobs. Justice's. The EMTs telling Dad that they were going to move Mom outside. The cops shuffling around the house. I wanted to rip my ears off. I wanted to scream at everyone to shut up. I didn't even realize I'd started scratching and yanking my ears until Dad touched my hand.

I flinched away. Disgusted with him. With myself. With the cops for being so goddamned noisy while my entire world imploded around me.

"Dad." Justice reached out a trembling hand. He took it and pulled her up into a hug. She slumped into him and cried more.

I didn't move.

When a short, stout cop asked me what happened ten minutes later, her pen poised over her notepad, I said, "It was a wolf." That was it. The words rang hollow to my ears. She wrote it down and left me alone, sitting on the floor.

I made myself as small as I could, hugging my knees to my chest and wrapping my arms tightly around my shins. This was all too much. I dug my nails into my flesh until I couldn't take the pain. My pajamas, a pair of old basketball shorts and a thin camisole, left me feeling exposed, so I shuffled until I found a corner to disappear into.

None of the cops asked about the salt, now scattered around the room. Only Dad's friend George Lyon, a detective with the St. Louis PD, asked any actual questions but made no comment on how Dad cleaned up a crime scene or about the blood on his clothes. When a uniformed cop asked why they weren't taking Dad to the station, Detective Lyon told them to search the backyard for any sign of a wolf. They looked like they wanted to argue, but the detective shot them a menacing glare, and the cops did as instructed.

"Thanks for… everything," Dad whispered to his friend as most of the uniforms filed out of our damaged front door in search of a wolf they'd never find.

"Don't mention it." George squeezed Dad's shoulder. Standing side by side, he made Dad look excessively tall, which was a feat since Dad came in at five foot nine. "Everett, are you going to be okay here? I have half a mind to leave a squad car out front."

Dad's voice strained as he answered. "That won't be necessary."

"I know you can take care of yourself, but—" George stopped mid-sentence when he caught me watching their exchange. He rubbed his forehead. "Listen, you say this is handled, then I trust you."

"It's handled."

George, to his credit, only spent a silent five count before nodding. "You call me if that changes. And Mark said you and the girls are more than welcome to stay with us. He'd love a reason to make a five-course meal."

"Thanks. We'll be just fine."

The detective nodded once more before heading out the door to join the rest of his team.

Claiming he needed to help search for signs of the wolf, Dad grabbed his keys and left after the last squad car drove off. Morbidly, I wondered if he needed to get away from me.

Justice pulled herself together when the rumble of Dad's '77 Chevy Silverado faded. She gripped my shoulders, placing us eye to eye. "What happened? Dad's acting weird."

I didn't answer. My brain still stuck on how none of this could be real. We went into the kitchen, and she brewed coffee while I sat in silence at the kitchen table. I cried as the earthy smell of Mom's favorite dark roast fought the coppery smell of her death. A silent, motionless cry. Justice sat across from me. She'd poured us each a mug, but I didn't drink. The thought of enjoying Mom's favorite coffee made my insides feel greasy.

The mid-morning sun streamed in through the window over the sink, casting our shadows on the wall. I pictured Justice at age five, making shadow puppets in this kitchen with Dad. He'd just read to us from his book about The Jersey Devil, and Justice asked how it managed to get around so quickly. Dad took a flashlight from our junk drawer and showed her how the winged beast flew. Justice laughed, but I remember running out of the kitchen in search of Mom, Justice's giggles trailing after me.

I knew if Justice had been home, she wouldn't have frozen. She wouldn't have run from the truth like I did. No. She would have put the pieces together. Even if they didn't seem possible. Even if it was insane to consider one of Dad's stories had manifested *inside our living room.*

Her brain worked with facts, not "should be" or "shouldn't be."

And the fact was a wolf-man with superhuman abilities drained our mother's blood while I watched.

Our childhood had been full of stories about all things mystical and impossible, read to us like Mother Goose tales. Most came directly from Dad's own lecture series *American Lore,* books he wrote about urban myths and legends. And for some reason (a reason I now understand), afterward, he quizzed us. Out of spite, I never paid much attention, failing his little quizzes, refusing to play his "educational games," and dismissing his insistence on learning the weaknesses of fake creatures that I'd never see *because they weren't real.*

They weren't supposed to be real.

Justice treated it like school, complete with quizzes and flashcards. She knew almost as much as Dad, and he taught American Lore at colleges around the country. Not me. I hated those days when he sat us down to lecture us on the difference between a Vampire with an "I" and a Vampyr with a "Y."

My little sister, *she* hung on his every word. Memorized the stories. Even laid out salt under the windows and in front of our bedroom door to ward off bad spirits until she was thirteen. She would have instinctively realized what had crashed into the living room, mad with hunger, without a litany of denials. Of that much, I was sure.

"Prue."

Called back to reality by my sister's voice, I finally answered, "It wasn't a wolf." The words felt like chewing on barbed wire. I didn't want to say the words or — believe them.

"What was it?"

I shook my head, unable to say it. Running from trouble in my own mind.

"If it wasn't a wolf, then what?"

"A Rougarou," I choked out. The truth had solidified moments before Dad poured the salt circle around me. Even as I recognized the beast, my instincts were to deny it. Rougarous didn't exist. I had to be seeing things.

"*What?*"

"Don't make me say it again. Please."

Mercifully, Justice didn't. "You're not hurt, right?"

I stared down at the tiny slices on my palms. They'd stopped bleeding but looked angry and red. "I crawled. Broken vase."

Justice scrutinized the cuts a moment longer and, after a beat, sat down. "It must be okay. Otherwise, Dad would have told you, right?"

Her sudden shift from confusion to panic and then back to her usual stoicism made my head spin.

"Told me what?"

Justice's brow pinched together, and she propped her elbows on the table, steepling her fingers in a pose reminiscent of Sherlock Holmes. "Dad wouldn't have left if he thought you were infected." She said it like I'd avoided catching the flu and not a fucking mythical curse that would turn me into the same kind of monster that killed Mom. The thought sent a shiver through me.

I sure as hell felt cursed.

"If I remember right, you'd have shifted by now." She smiled, but it didn't quite reach her eyes. "Probably."

"It's not real." I waved my hand, attempting to dismiss the truth. "Those are just stories. The Rougarou is a myth. I can't believe this. It's not real." I rubbed my temples, willing myself to wake up from this nightmare.

"I know," Justice said.

I shoved to my feet and paced. "It's a legend. For God's sake, there's a Rougarou festival every year in New Orleans. It can't be *real* if there's a festival about it."

"I'm so sorry, Prue."

"No, it can't be a Rougarou."

"But it was. You said it yourself."

"That means all those times Dad assured us that nothing from his stories was real—he *lied*." I set my hands flat on the table, leaning down to look at Justice. Her brown, almond-shaped eyes, a perfect mirror of my own—of Mom's—glistened with unshed tears. "He *lied* to us, Justice. Our whole fucking lives. He lied."

A flush crept up Justice's neck, settling in her cheeks. She avoided looking at me, instead focusing on her mug. "I guess."

"It means he let us believe we were safe—that things like this don't happen, but they did. They do." My face grew hot, a fusion of anger and shame. "It happened, and because he lied, I stood there frozen thinking 'this isn't real'' while Mom died."

"There wasn't anything you could do…" Justice broke off, her sob masked as a cough. "You survived. That's what you did."

Yeah.

But Mom died.

When Dad got home hours later with assurances that the Rougarou had left town, he told us "the truth."

"I'm not *just* a lecturer," he said after he grabbed a Diet Coke and cracked it open. He leaned against the sink rather than sitting at the table with us.

I noticed lines around his eyes, deep as riverbeds, and the pasty, sallow color of his usually tanned skin. Normally, he managed to look boyish, even at fifty, with his long black hair in a braid. Not today.

"Dad, what does that mean exactly?" Justice asked, a slight tremble in her voice.

"I hunt things like the Rougarou." A line formed between his brows, hardening his expression. "I have for a while. You know how I lost my family in that car accident?"

Justice nodded.

"That's only part of it. When I was seventeen, we were on a family road trip. This time to the Badlands. Your grandmother loved national parks," he stared down at his boots and cleared his throat, "when we were camping, something happened."

Justice sat raptly, eyes wide and lips pursed, as she took in every word. I resented her ability to compartmentalize. Part of her mourned Mom while another listened to Dad.

All of me raged. It seared into me with each syllable he uttered.

"Dad was off helping my brother go to the bathroom when Mom suddenly jumped up from where she'd been roasting marshmallows and asked if I heard something. I told her I hadn't, but she was convinced. She moved so fast. Like her body wasn't hers anymore. I called for Dad, but she was gone by the time he and Nathan got back.

"We searched on foot for hours. Nathan was only ten, so Dad and I both held his hands. I don't even remember letting go or sprinting off. I just remember a scream. One that chilled me to my soul. I ran toward it.

"Dad and Nathan shouted for me to come back, but I kept running. That's when I saw it. A Banshee, pale with eyes like coal. I didn't know that then, of course. Its clawed hands ripped my mom to shreds as she wailed. I shouted for her, and the Banshee stopped, tilted her head at me, and snapped my mom's neck. I blacked out after that."

"How did you survive?" Justice asked.

"I woke up on a cot in some office with an older woman sitting in a chair watching me. I screamed and fought her until I collapsed. She let me. Finally, when I calmed down, she explained that she was a park ranger. She found me. My family, all of them, were dead."

"Why did you lie about how they died?" I asked, cutting him off. Sadness clouded his features at my question. Guilt eased past my rage at the sight of his bloodshot eyes and tear-stained cheeks. I shoved it aside.

"The woman who rescued me, Anne, taught me about Banshees and everything else that should have only been stories told around a campfire. She taught me how to protect myself and, most importantly, that I was to forget it ever happened and get on with my life, so I tried. I went to college in the fall and managed to almost believe the story that my family died in a car crash. I met your mom, and things started to feel normal."

"But?" Justice asked.

"But normal didn't last long. I always kept an eye on news coming out of the Badlands. One day, I read a story about someone who went through something similar and went back to find Anne. She was pissed at first, telling me to get on with my life, but eventually, she taught me how to do what she did. I couldn't help my family, but I could make sure others didn't lose everything, like I had."

Fresh tears ran down his cheeks. I couldn't remember the last time I'd seen Dad cry. It made him look small, and somehow that pissed me off. His ice-blue eyes turned heavenward as he answered. "I didn't want you to grow up looking everywhere for danger, but I needed you to recognize it if it showed up, so I taught you, hoping I'd never have to tell you why."

"Did Mom know?" Justice surprised me by asking the question before I could.

"Not at first," he admitted.

"When?"

"I told her after Prue was born. She didn't believe me." He shook his head at the memory. "You know how she is — was — always so stubborn, but I needed her to believe me because I needed you both to be safe when I was… out of town."

I fought the urge to shout and asked, "You ever consider not leaving town?"

"Yes, God, yes. Of course. I told anyone who knew me that I was out. Done. I had a family, but monsters don't care. People I'd helped called or gave my contact information to someone who needed my help. I ignored them until your mother started asking why I didn't lecture anymore even though so many universities called." He paused for a moment, gathering himself. "I picked colleges to visit based on occurrences that seem 'other.' When all of a sudden, I was home all the time, your mom grew curious."

I wanted to scream and upend the table and rage, rage, rage. I didn't. I managed to keep myself together, clenching my fists at my sides. "And she agreed to keep this from us?"

"Yes, at least until Justice finished high school. We wanted to wait for the right time. For when you were both settled, but then we kept coming up with reasons we shouldn't tell you. I think, well, I think neither of us wanted to taint the way you two saw the world — the constant looking over your shoulder. Always on alert. I took jobs that were far away. I guess I convinced myself that I could keep the two things separate.

"That there wouldn't be blowback if I kept it far enough away. Some of the things I hunted were unthinking, primal things that couldn't form a coherent thought, but others, like the Rougarou, held onto a semblance of consciousness. I thought, as long as I made sure nothing could track me home, everything would be alright."

"Jesus Christ, Dad," I snapped, slamming my clenched fists on the table. "Jesus Fucking Christ."

Justice gasped, recoiling from my unexpected violence.

For most of the conversation, Dad took my accusations in stride, but now his jaw set in a hard line, and his eyes narrowed. His tone remained even as he said, "It was to protect you."

"Well, look how well that worked out."

I knew it was cruel. I said it anyway.

"Prue, that's not fair," Justice said.

"Fair? *Fair*?" I tasted bile, acrid, and burning. "Is it fair that Mom died because Dad was off saving someone else? Is it fair that he left us unguarded by lying to us? Is that fair, Justice?"

Her lip trembled, and I hated myself for it, but I couldn't contain my rage—at myself, Dad, the Rougarou… at Mom.

"If you always worked far away from home, how did it find us?"

The Dad who was always so sure of himself shriveled away. I could see it in the hunch of his shoulders, in the twitching of his mouth as he tried to find the words.

"Scent."

"How?"

"I stopped at a gas station at the Arkansas border. Some back-country place with one pump. A woman screamed loud enough that I heard her over the downpour. I couldn't ignore it. I stopped the Rougarou from biting her, but it got away. I shot it. I interfered with its meal. I… I pissed it off."

"And so, it came to find you?" Justice sounded unsteady, as if she were attempting to ask questions while walking a tightrope. "It wanted… revenge?"

"Like I said, Rougarous hold onto some of their human emotions. It had my scent, it was angry, so it tracked me. The rain and all the mud should have been enough to mask me, but it's so much faster than a car..." Dad succumbed to his exhaustion and grief, sliding to the floor. He pulled his legs up and hugged himself. "I called, but your mom didn't answer. I tried to get here in time."

Justice moved to his side, placing a hand over his. "Dad, you got here in time to keep Prue safe."

Dad raised his gaze to meet mine. "It's still out there."

"Will it come back?" I asked, refusing to be affected by his tears.

"I couldn't find any trace of it in town or the surrounding areas. I shot it twice with rock salt—one in the leg and one in its shoulder. The salt burns them like acid. The human side won't even know why they're in pain when it shifts back."

"So, we're okay for now? While it heals, right?" Justice asked, her tone matter of fact.

"Not necessarily," Dad said. "But it's wounded. There's a good chance it will go somewhere familiar to heal. Most Rougarous come out of Louisiana. It's their territory. That's where the first curse occurred sometime in the 1800s, and since they prefer swamps to cities, the curse usually stays local to the region. I wasn't expecting to see one so far north."

I bit back the impulse to accuse Justice of treating this like a pop quiz and instead asked, "How are you so calm?"

"I'm not," she said.

"Could have fooled me." Instant regret filled me when I saw my sister's eyes well up. Hurting Justice, hurting Dad… letting Mom die. Jesus, I was on a roll today.

"You're not the only one who lost Mom, Prue." Justice rubbed her eyes with the heel of her palms.

"I'm… Justice… I'm sorry. It's just, aren't you even a little pissed that they kept this secret from us all this time while waiting for some random 'right' time to drop the bomb that 'hey, there are monsters in the world, just FYI.' Think about if we knew, if I knew..." My chest tightened as shame ripped past my rage, crashing through me. "If I knew, I could hav—could have..."

The rest of what I said came out in unintelligible sobs. I sank into myself, covering my face with my hands. My throat burned as I dry heaved through a coughing fit. Out of my periphery, I saw Dad moving toward me with an outstretched hand.

"No." I shoved back from my chair and pointed my finger at him. I staggered toward the door to the garage, my body tight with unstable rage, and turned my back on him and Justice. "I don't deserve it, anyway."

Before anyone could argue, I pushed the door open and stepped into the darkness.

I refused to think about Dad. I refused to feel bad.

I climbed into my beat-up Lincoln Town car, which used to be Mom's, and reclined the driver's seat. I used to come out here as a kid whenever I got upset. Sitting in the driver's seat, I would pretend I was driving far away. Dad wanted to scrap it, but Mom kept it for me and fixed it up as a present for my eighteenth birthday.

Safe inside the twilit haven of my car, I cried. When my tears trailed off, I sat in silence, staring at the liner of the Lincoln's roof. I had no idea how much time had passed, but my throat felt raw, so I figured it had been a while.

My head rolled toward the door to the house as it creaked open.

"Prue?" Justice's voice reverberated in the darkness before the light switch clicked. I heard a low hum as the bare bulb above the car illuminated everything.

"Here."

After a beat, the passenger door opened. She looked hesitant, and I hated how that felt.

"Can we talk?" she asked, getting in.

I laughed, a scratchy, mirthless sound. "Always."

"I think I blame him, too," she said. "A little part of me, at least."

"Really?" I tried to keep the disbelief out of my voice but failed. I'd never heard her disagree with Dad before. Not even that summer he ruined her birthday party by refusing to let her best friend's mom give her a "fairy cake." He never said why; he'd thrown the cake away in front of everyone. Mom had been shocked but didn't protest. Justice cried for a week, and then it was over. She never mentioned it again.

"He knows all these things about the world. What it's really like." She shook her head. "I mean, how were we supposed to be prepared if we thought it was all fairy tales and bedtime stories? We never… I took him seriously in a scholarly way, but not in a 'this can actually happen' way. Like, even if I was here, would I have remembered the salt thing in time? You're right. He left us underprepared."

"I'm sorry, Justice."

"No," she said. Like it was final. Like there wasn't room to argue. Her 'no' was a locked box, and I didn't have the key. "You have nothing to be sorry for. Nothing."

I bit my lip until I tasted blood. I couldn't handle it. Her forgiving me. Just like that. She gave me an out. A pass. She wasn't going to ask questions. Wouldn't make me relive it.

I didn't take it.

"I froze. I didn't get what was happening until it howled. Its mouth... it opened so wide, and the teeth were human but not. Sharper."

Justice remained silent beside me, letting me talk.

"Then I saw the eyes. So red. I looked at them, and they felt oddly human. Oval-shaped. What a stupid thing to remember." I swallowed, feeling my guilt surge. If Justice had been there, she'd have done something. Even if she forgot about the salt. She'd have done *something*. "I screamed, and Mom shoved me toward the kitchen. After that, it's a blur. Her body... I wish Dad had killed it. I wish he'd moved right past me without making sure that stupid salt circle was intact and shot the thing before it finished..."

"No," Justice snapped. "Don't say that. Don't."

"I'm sorry," I told her, "for what I said before. I didn't mean it."

She waved me off. "I... borrowed... this from Dad's office." She pulled the master copy of one of Dad's books from under her sweater. Dad kept hard copies of every draft he wrote. They were what he used on our weekend forays into fun games like 'let's pretend you're facing a pixie and they offer you some food; what do you do?'

"*Borrowed*? He keeps them in a locked file cabinet. You don't know how to pick locks."

"Yes, borrowed. And YouTube can teach you anything." She pushed her seat upright. "I found his entry on Rougarous, his unedited one, and there's something that didn't make it into the published version."

Justice had always come across as older than me. Everything about her was sharp — high cheekbones and a resting murder face that Charlize Theron would approve of. The only thing that made her look her age were her eyes. They betrayed her by being soft, honey-brown, and inquisitively doe-eyed.

She sounded intense, so I also put my seat up. "What?"

"There's mention of someone who can… well, they can locate a specific Rougarou. Dad refers to them as L.B. from Seville, Louisiana. It's crossed out with a sticky note that says: L.B. refused to be in the book."

I'd heard of that town before. Something in the back of my mind rattled loose as I tried to remember why it sounded familiar. Something from one of Dad's lessons, no doubt. Something about ley lines?

"It's a nexus," she informed me, and the memory solidified.

Ley line nexuses were places that had (according to lore) higher-than-usual reported sightings of unnatural phenomena. In the 1800s, Seville had a rash of brutal animal attacks.

Rougarou attacks.

I grabbed the manuscript, and Justice let me. I squinted at the page, tactfully ignoring the sketch. There wasn't much else written down, just the initials and location with two brief sentences reading: *Location spell worked. Reversing the curse didn't.*

"They can locate it?" I asked, too aware of the hope oozing out of my voice. "We need to find them."

Justice looked confused. "Prue, I didn't mean for us to do this. We should ask Dad to do it. Beg him if we have to. I know he said he didn't want to leave in case it came back, but—"

"No," I told her, and my 'no' was a locked box, too. "He lied. For years. How can I ever trust him again? How can you?" Knowing someone could help find this thing—I couldn't sit back and not go after it. I wanted to find it. I wanted to punish it. I wanted to end this sinking feeling.

"Okay, say we go to Seville. Find this person. Find the Rougarou. Then what?"

"Kill it."

Justice laughed, not unkindly. She laughed like she thought we should both laugh. Like I'd made a joke. When I didn't join her, she stopped. "You're serious?"

I snapped the manuscript closed. "You don't have to come, but I'm going. I did nothing to help Mom. I can't keep doing nothing."

Justice searched my face, scrutinizing me like a particularly dense bit of academic text. Whatever conclusion she drew from her search must have convinced her. "Okay, ignoring the fact that we have no real idea what we are doing, that the Rougarou could be anywhere, and that this contact of Dad's could be gone or dead for all we know — what's your plan to kill it? You ever chop something's head off?" She tapped the pages in my hand. "Because that's how it says to kill a Rougarou. We'd need, like, a chainsaw or something."

I shrugged and looked at the workbench where Dad's tools hung. My gaze went to the machete. "We'll take that."

"So that's the plan? Get Dad's machete and cut its head off?"

"Not dying would also be part of the plan."

"Alright, let's go tell Dad we are leaving in the morning to hunt the Rougarou. No biggie. Be back in a jiff." Sarcasm dripped off every syllable. When she was done theatrically rolling her eyes, she looked at me.

"I'm not telling him." I knew I sounded crazy, but finally, my rage had something to latch onto, something to steady me, and I couldn't let go.

Justice's eyes went squinty. Her thinking/concentrating/planning face. "We have to tell him something. The funeral won't be for a week, so there's some time for..." She nodded once, then cocked her head to the side. "That could work, for a day at least." She fished her phone out of her shorts pocket. The blue light cast her features in shadow. "A twelve-hour drive. Factor in... yeah, that works. Okay. I'm in."

"What works?" My sister often had conversations half in her head and half out loud. Most of the time, forgetting that she hadn't said the whole thing.

"We better pack. I'll tell Dad we are going to Aunt Penny's until the funeral and that we'll all drive back together in a few days. Aunt Penny might even cover for us if we leave out the Rougarou bit. She lives in the opposite direction, but the time on the road is similar-ish. No one will realize where we went for a while."

"No. We should leave tonight before he can convince us to stay home."

"Ah, see, that's the brilliant part. The tracks indicated it went south out of St. Louis. If we take some precautions—new clothes, lots of odor neutralizer, and body spray—I'm sure he'd be glad to have us further away from danger. As he said, they don't usually leave Louisiana, so the further from there, the better."

"You're okay with this? With lying to him?"

"If you blame yourself for freezing, you have to know I blame myself for not even being there."

I wanted to refuse, but she raised her eyebrows, daring me to deny her guilt after I'd let mine explode across the kitchen like a grenade. Wisely, I kept my mouth shut.

She offered me a hesitant smile before looking down at Dad's book. "We should photograph important bits and put this back, so Dad doesn't know we took it."

"*We?*"

Justice scowled and stuck out her tongue before turning back to the book. She called up her camera app and clicked away. After several minutes, my phone dinged as she forwarded the shots.

Closing the book, she hesitated before getting out. "I'm packing CDs. I refuse to listen to country radio the whole way." And then she was gone. Inside the house to pack for both of us.

I sat in the car for a moment. Trying to push away the image of Mom's limp form tossed over the couch like a throw blanket. I failed, and more tears ripped through me, but I didn't feel so helpless this time.

Chapter Two

Dad waved goodbye from the shattered door as we pulled out of the driveway—still in a dirty wrestling shirt with an expression a little like relief hidden under fatherly concern. He'd tried to convince us to stay home, but Dad never had the heart to deny Justice anything. Especially not after she pulled the "it will be good for us to get out of the house until the funeral" card.

So off we went to find the wizard, witch, or whatever they considered themselves. Either way, I was ready to barrel down the yellow brick road until I found them and convinced them to help us.

"Okay, I texted Aunt Penny. She's still good with 'avoiding the truth,' as she put it. She sent a heart emoji and said for us to blow off some steam."

"I feel kinda bad lying to her," I admitted. Mom's younger sister held the black sheep title in Mom's family. I'd always adored her. When we'd explained that we needed some time away from everything that reminded us of Mom, Aunt Penny immediately understood, agreeing to cover for us once we promised to check in.

Justice eyed me. "For real? It's the least shitty thing we're doing."

She had a point.

"Turn off the Find-Your-Friend app," Justice told me as we rounded the corner, losing sight of Dad. "I don't think he'll try it, but just in case."

"You still sure?" I asked for the hundredth time. Justice had never gone against Dad this absolutely. I needed to know it wasn't a fluke, that she wouldn't duck out or narc on us halfway through.

"Prue, how many times do you want me to say I'm with you on this?"

"You don't have to come, you know. Dad and I are already on shaky terms at best. I'm fine with him being pissed at me." I gave her a side-eyed glance. "Can you tell me you're okay with that?"

Justice shuffled in her seat, sinking further down and propping her feet on the dash. "No, I'm not okay with it, but I'm not okay with doing nothing, so… I'm in."

"Swear it. Do it. Swear. Like when we were kids."

"Come on? Really?"

"Really."

Justice sighed. "I, Justice Lynn Wells, swear to my big sister, Prudence Ann Wells, that I won't be a little brat and tell Dad what we are up to." She waited a moment before adding, "Happy?"

"Very."

I pushed one of my CDs into the player and laughed as Justice let out a groan. We fought for a moment over the volume, but I won, and Kelly Clarkson's "Breakaway" rattled through my ancient speakers as we zipped onto the highway.

"Well, that could have gone better." I ducked as a chicken wing soared over my head. I followed its descent—*splat*—as it landed on the windshield of the Lincoln.

"I'm gonna have glitter on me forever," Justice said, vainly brushing at her shirt. Another chicken wing whizzed past her.

"You're banned," the owner of Sweet Lou's Gentlemen's Club shouted at us, tossing two more All-You-Can-Eat Buffalo wings at my car. "Banned."

I flipped her the bird without turning around and hit the button to unlock the car.

"Seriously?" Justice picked up a wing, grimaced, then tossed it over her shoulder.

I crossed my eyes and stuck my tongue out. Justice returned with a spectacularly exaggerated eye roll. After ten hours on the road together, we had regressed into adolescence, which seemed par for the course since we smelled like middle school boys about to go to their first dance. The amount of AXE Body Spray we'd used to mask our scents from the Rougarou should be illegal, or at least count as the eighth deadly sin.

I got in while Justice finished clearing off the wings. My car might smell like buffalo sauce, and I would shed glitter until I died, but we'd gotten what we came for: Seville lay thirty miles south.

It had been a shock when Justice tried putting Seville into Google Maps and got an error message. According to the big old Google in the sky, Seville didn't exist. At least not on the internet. Four crappy roadside gas stations with *Evil Dead* vibes and one Gentlemen's club later, and we had a map with Seville on it and an actual idea of how to get there.

Google, eat shit and die.

Sweat rolled down my spine, and I desperately longed for the club's cold, dark, air-conditioned haven. Even leaving the windows down did nothing to lessen the heat in the car's interior.

"You suck," Justice said, sliding into the passenger seat.

"And you smell like hot sauce."

She rolled her eyes. "I can't believe how hard this freaking town is to find."

"We got it now," I told her. The engine turned over with the effort of a car that'd seen too many miles and not enough maintenance. "Seville's south. There's a weird dirt road to take. Et voila."

Justice pulled out her phone and searched the GPS for what lay south. "Nothing but one small town on the way. Oh, and a big-ass swamp."

Sometimes my sister's need for everything to go 'just so' drove me nuts. She cranked the air up to the highest setting and leaned close to the vent pretending the hot air being pushed out was better than the hot air coming in from the windows.

"Are we gonna go, or...?"

I gave a mock salute. "Yes, ma'am."

Her eyes crinkled at the corners, but she held her mouth in a firm line. I scrutinized her face: the obstinate set of her jaw, the pulsing vein in her forehead, and her flaring nostrils. She looked too much like Mom when she was frustrated. A memory tried to force its way to the forefront of my mind, but with a stubborn will, I shoved it away.

"Prue, is everything…"

I drummed my fingers on the steering wheel. "So, south?"

"Yeah, south."

Mercifully, Justice didn't pry. She started to compare the directions on her phone to the paper map, but her screen lit up with an incoming call and Dad's picture. A good one of him from our last-ever family vacation to Disney. He wore Princess Leia buns.

Justice sighed as she hit ignore. "This is the fifth time today. Aunt Penny texted when we were in the club. She said 'S.O.S.' then texted about three hundred alarm emojis."

I didn't say anything because everything that came to my mind was unkind. Justice might be with me on this, but she didn't like hurting Dad. I could respect that, even if I didn't have the same reservation at the moment.

"Let's hope L.B. is easier to find than Seville." I put the car in drive and listened to Justice resume complaints about my shitty taste in late 90s-early 2000s pop music as she told me which turn to take.

⸏⸎⸏

"We're lost," Justice informed me for the fifth time in as many minutes. The backroads of Louisiana were endless. Who knew? And thanks to dozens of trees covered in Spanish moss, every road looked the same in the inky blackness. My Lincoln's dim headlights didn't help matters. And the cicadas' low hum drowned out Alanis Morrisette singing about irony. An owl joined the eerie symphony, perfecting the picture with a hellish hoot.

I pinched the bridge of my nose. "As helpful as it is for you to keep reminding me, maybe take a break and reset the GPS. We can find a motel and look for this dirt road again in the daylight."

My sister, to her credit, responded with only a slightly passive-aggressive *harumph* before punching in Tomas's Hollow, the small town we passed through less than an hour ago.

While she did that, I drove without direction down the dark country road for an infinite moment, only able to see a foot in front of the car. "Would it kill them to put in street lights?"

"No signal." She held up her phone as proof—the blue light on the screen an unwelcome brightness for my night-adjusted eyes.

"Perfect."

"Ugh," she said, and I felt like that pretty much summed up our situation.

"Well, what next? Follow the dark road until we run out of gas? That's not the opening to a horror movie or anything." My tone could have used an attitude adjustment, but I couldn't keep my irritation in check. On top of everything, my stomach growled, begging me to find something edible, or else it was prepared to initiate Full-Meltdown-Mode.

"Whatever," Justice said, her tone's attitude only slightly less tetchy. She raked a hand through her hair. "I'm tired."

"Do we have anything to eat? I'd even suffer through one of your gross power bars. I'm that starving."

"Seriously?" There was an edge to her voice, and I realized she wasn't just cranky-I-want-out-of-this-car tired. She was this-is-insane-what-was-I-thinking tired.

"What's wrong?" It was the dumbest question in existence. Of course, I knew what was wrong. Mom was dead.

"You accuse me of being too calm back at the house, and yet we are driving into a literal abyss," she said, pointing out at the dark road, "and you want a snack?"

"Wow."

"Wow." She scrunched her face and mocked me. "I mean, shit, we're lost, okay? And Dad, Christ, he's called so many times. I just don't know how you aren't freaking out. Like *you're* the freak-out queen, yet here I am… freaking out."

I clenched the steering wheel and heard the plastic squeak under strain. "I can't."

"Can't what?"

"Freak out. If I let myself think about it. If I stop long enough to be sad, angry, or scared, I'll break, and I don't know if I could pull it back together."

I felt her hand warm on my shoulder. "I didn't…"

"I just need this, okay? I need to keep moving, and I need you to keep moving with me. Okay?"

There was a moment of quiet before she said, "Okay."

"Right." I cleared my throat and licked the salty tears off my upper lip. "So, are there any nasty, healthy power bars left?"

The agitation that had filled the car over the last hour burst. Justice punched me on the shoulder, not hard enough to leave a bruise but enough that I swerved. She looked down at her feet and then the middle console —home to our two big gulps of cherry soda. No power bars in sight. "Where did you put them?"

"Backseat, I think."

"You mean the black hole you call a backseat?"

"Yup."

"Will you ever clean it?"

"Not likely."

"Glad we cleared that up."

Justice reclined her chair and did a sort of contortionist's movement, so she lay belly down on the seat and rummaged through the junk in the back.

"We will hit civilization eventually, right?" I could tell she was still upset by the slight tremble in her voice. Maybe not at me anymore, but our argument wasn't over.

"Not if we went through some kind of portal and are doomed to drive on this infernal road for eternity," I added a poor imitation of the *Twilight Zone* theme, which made me laugh but made her groan.

"You sure know how to lighten the mood."

Thank fuck, she sounded less upset. "It's a talent."

"Jesus, Prue, I love you and everything, but I just saw a *Seventeen Magazine* with Zac Efron on the cover from 2008. And I swear to God, I don't want to know, but why do you have a 2-liter bottle filled with what looks like blood?"

"Halloween. Remember Carrie?"

"That was five years ago."

I laughed at her affronted act. We used to share a room, and it was more of the same. I didn't care where I dropped my socks. She would wax poetic about hampers. You know, sibling stuff.

"Oh, got 'em," she said triumphantly, then, "Dude, that's where those Lego went?" She sat upright and tossed the bag of power bars at me without looking. "I cried when I thought I lost Obi-Wan's mini-fig, and you just have him in here with a bunch of random bricks."

"My bad," I said, ripping the power bar open with my teeth. "Forgot it was there."

"I'm taking these," she said, hugging the bag of Lego to her chest like she had found the holy grail.

"Coolio," I mumbled as I chewed.

"Ew, decorum much." Justice tucked the bag of Lego into her messenger bag and grabbed a power bar.

"Sorry, Ms. Manners, I forgot I was amongst royalty."

Justice huffed out a chuckle. "This isn't crazy, right?"

"It's for Mom," I reminded her. And maybe a bit for myself, but I didn't have time to think too hard about that.

We drove aimlessly, squinting into the darkness for any sign of a dirt road in the endless night. A flash of movement streaked in front of the headlights. I slammed on the brakes with both feet, lurching the car. My seatbelt cut into my chest. I swore, using some choice words that daytime television would have bleeped out.

"Deer?" Justice leaned forward, looking out the windshield. "It looked huge."

"Whatever it was, I almost hit it." My fingers rubbed the sore spot on my collarbone. I unbuckled. My neck stung, raw from the burn of the fabric.

"I officially hate backroads," Justice informed me. I grunted in agreement. Lifting my foot off the brake pedal, I shifted to the gas, creeping forward cautiously, but before I could get up to full speed, the sound of sirens made me jump.

"Are we getting pulled over?" Justice twisted in her seat to look back. "Where did they even come from?"

The sirens whooped again. I pulled over, tensing as I tried to figure out what I had done wrong. Next to me, Justice had AXE spray in one hand and a canister of salt in the other. I'd have laughed if I wasn't so freaking relieved she came with me.

I put the car in park, and from the rearview mirror, I saw a cop get out and don a cowboy-type hat before striding over to the passenger side. One hand resting on a holstered gun, the other resting on the walkie attached to their shoulder.

Justice rolled her window down, not bothering to release the salt or Axe spray, holding them at a low angle. "Hello, officer."

The cop bent down to peer inside the car. "Y'all know why I pulled you over?" Her features were hard to distinguish under the hat's brim, but her voice had that mellifluous southern lilt that made me think of sweet tea, porch swings, and lightning bugs.

"Were we doing something wrong, officer?" I asked. "I don't think I was speeding."

As we waited for an answer, a second squad car pulled up, and another cop ambled over. Whoever they were, they hadn't bothered with lights or sirens, arriving in near silence. In comic contrast to the first cop, this one was short and round. When he reached us, I noted a graying push-broom mustache that matched a pair of bushy eyebrows on a wrinkled face.

Brandishing a small flashlight, the new cop peered at us. "Howdy, I'm Sheriff Rose. And y'all are?"

"Justice Wells," Justice supplied.

"So, what? Tail Light out? Brake Light? Is there even a reason why you pulled us over?" I asked.

"Sorry, officers, my sister doesn't mean to be rude. We've managed to get ourselves a little lost, and it's been frustrating."

"License and registration."

I grabbed the documents from the middle console and fished my license out of my wallet, passing everything to the cop.

The first cop scanned the documents. "From St. Louis? That's quite a drive. What brings you out this way?"

"Are we getting a ticket, or... can we go?"

Justice's low groan confirmed how poorly this social exchange was going, as if I didn't already know. She cleared her throat. "Sorry, officers, but why did you stop us, if you don't mind my asking?"

"Routine stop," the sheriff answered. He sounded like John Wayne if he were an optimist. "We're looking for someone known to steal cars, and your plates came up stolen, but I see all your paperwork is in order, so there must be some mistake?"

Fuck! Of course, Dad had Detective Lyon report my car stolen when he couldn't get ahold of us, just like he'd convinced Lyon to tell everyone Mom's death had been a tragic but isolated animal attack. How long had Dad trusted his friend with the truth?

I plastered my best 'don't look at me' smile across my face and left Justice to answer. Best I kept my mouth shut. The next words to come out were bound to be nasty.

Justice answered with a quick lie. "We're visiting an old family friend. In Seville. Our dad's probably worried that we didn't check in yet, but the service out here is crap, and in the dark, it's hard to spot the road into town."

"That it is," the first cop agreed. "I'm Officer Hoyt. How about you two follow me, so we can get this sorted."

"Are you going to report that you found us?" I asked, pushing the words out slowly, willing them to sound nonchalant. "Because once we get service, we can just call our dad."

Officer Hoyt laughed, not unkindly, but certainly not like she was keen on fulfilling my request. "Come on, I'll bring you to Mo's Diner so we can chat. It's closer than the station and has the benefit of coffee that tastes like it's supposed to."

It wasn't the answer I was looking for, but what choice did we have? Kind of odd she was taking us to a diner and not the police station, but my stomach, for one, wasn't complaining. Besides, if it got us to Seville, it was the first luck we had on this trip. "Sure."

"I'm going to keep searching for a while more," Sheriff Rose said. He gave Hoyt a look heavy with meaning. "I'll radio if I find anything."

Hoyt nodded once, looking like she hated the idea of leaving him alone. "See that you do, sheriff."

With that settled, we drove off. I watched the sheriff in my rearview and saw him heading into the woods, flashlight in one hand and gun in the other. I didn't know much about being a cop, but I didn't think he would find the car thief in a swamp.

After a few miles, Hoyt put on her blinker, and I barely caught the glint of a road sign proclaiming: *Seville Next Right*. I've no clue how we would have spotted it on our own, but I took the turn.

In the distance, red neon lights shone, proclaiming we had arrived at Mo's Diner. Most 24-hour restaurants felt like they existed in the same pocket of the universe. Step in, and the bell rings to announce all arrivals. A coffee pot sizzles. Cutlery clinks. Someone shouts for another order of fries, followed by the bubbly squish of a ketchup bottle and change clattering on the countertop to join the never-ending chorus.

Mo's seemed no different.

Situated between a 1960s motel that looked like it had been shoved through a wormhole and a grandiose expanse of murky swamp land, Mo's boasted the best pancakes in Louisiana with an offering of thirty possible toppings.

I parked next to Hoyt's squad car, feeling overly self-conscious—did I always turn the lights off before I put the car in park? Should I have used a turn signal to get into the spot? Did I even know how to drive?

Justice nudged me. "C'mon."

I took two deep breaths and turned the ignition off. When I looked out my window, I saw Hoyt staring in. In the red neon light, her features came into half-view. Hawk-ish nose with narrow eyes to match. Skin the color of dark coffee. Lips pursed—looking for all the world like every small-town cop I'd ever seen on a TV show.

Justice shoved her can of AXE in front of me as I unbuckled and hit me with a generous spritz of Epic Sky, which made my eyes water. She sprayed herself, too, then put the canister in her messenger bag along with the salt.

If Hoyt thought we were being weird, I couldn't tell. She stood patiently, hands on hips, waiting. The officer wrinkled her nose but didn't mention how pungent Justice and I smelled in the muggy night air. "Let's get you two some coffee, yeah?"

Despite the sinking feeling in my gut—had Hoyt already reported in, letting Dad know exactly where we were? — the promise of coffee perked me up.

The aesthetic in Mo's walked the line between a dive bar and your middle school best friend's mom's kitchen. What were clearly family photos hung on the wall above and behind the counter, intermixed with autographed photos of small-time celebrities and snapshots of several years' worth of little league teams with Mo's emblazoned across their shirts.

The few people sitting at the counter craned their necks when we stepped inside. I must've scowled because the rent-a-cop lifting a forkful of pancake shot me his best 'we don't like outsiders' sneer before he nodded at Hoyt. I'd have cared if my stomach wasn't suddenly demanding my full attention.

"Hiya, Charline," said a middle-aged woman with a stained apron. She had cherry-red hair and lips to match. "Y'all want a booth?"

I turned to Justice and mouthed, "*Charline*?" To which she shrugged and rolled her eyes.

"Mo here?"

The redhead smiled big, and it was surprisingly charming. "In the back. Gary called out. Mary's in labor. Can you believe? Two months early."

"Go ahead and get them a booth." Hoyt turned to us, putting the full weight of her hawkish gaze on us. "I'll be back in a minute to sort you out."

Justice nodded. "Okay."

"I'm Lorrie," the woman said when we were alone. She led us to an empty booth away from the prying eyes at the counter. "Where about y'all from?" I tensed, but she smiled softly. "It's a small town. You tend to assume anyone you don't recognize is from somewhere else."

"St. Louis," I answered as Justice said, "Missouri."

Lorrie raised a brow. "You do that a lot? Talk at the same time?"

I shrugged. Justice smiled her best 'teacher's pet' smile. "Sisters. You know how it is."

"Do I ever?" Lorrie's mouth curved into another smile. "I'm the youngest of six. All girls. My mamma spent half her life trying to get us to leave one another be. The other half she spent trying to figure out why Daddy left. No mystery, that. Anyone in their right mind would've run for the hills after seeing six teenage girls sharing one bathroom."

Lorrie rattled on about her family, and Justice listened like she might actually remember the names of all five of Lorrie's sisters. I reclined back into the squeaky seat and scanned the place. Lorrie sat us near the swinging door that led to the kitchen. I could just make out the sounds of a conversation over the clanking of pans.

Hoyt must've told Dad she'd found us. I mean, she's a cop, so she'd have to report that she found a stolen car. Dad would be on his way here. And it would all be over. He'd never let us find L.B., let alone the Rougarou. How could it just be over?

"…well, anyway, that's what I get for trying," Lorrie said, and it felt like the end of a story, so I interjected before another could begin. "Can we see some menus?"

Might as well drown my sorrows in greasy diner food. Those power bars Justice loved hardly counted as food.

"Of course, sweetheart." Lorrie didn't waste a second running over to the counter and grabbing two thick, laminated menus. "Now, our specialty is pancakes. In case the signs and huge pictures of pancakes didn't make that clear." Her eyes crinkled at the corners. "I prefer Nutella and bananas, myself. Mo never skimps on the Nutella when she's on the grill."

Now, Lorrie had my attention. "Hell yeah, that." I handed the menu back without opening it. At least I'd be stuffed with coffee and pancakes when Dad caught up with us and launched into a lecture about how stupid we were for chasing after the Rougarou.

Justice did a mock gag that went out of style in third grade and opened the menu. It took up the whole table. "I'll have the egg white veggie omelet and a side of wheat toast."

"Easy peasy. Anything to drink?"

"Coffee," we said in unison, earning us another easy smile from Lorrie and her cherry-red lips.

"You two are a kick." She grabbed the menus and went through the swinging door. I got a glimpse of the kitchen. Some guy sat on a countertop filming another kid as he performed some kind of monologue. I turned back to Justice, and she sighed down at her phone.

"My phone service is still spotty. This is a whole ass mess." She waved her arms around like those inflatable men at used car lots. "And how the hell are you still so hungry?"

I pulled my phone out of my back pocket. No bars. "Probably not many towers. We did have to take a dirt road to get here, and to your other questions: I'm always hungry, and yeah, this is a certified mess."

"Maybe there's Wi-Fi?"

"Yeah, and maybe Santa is real."

"Actually, he is real," Justice said. To my utter dismay, she looked perfectly serious. "Well, a version, anyway. Yule spirit. If Rougarous are real, most of the stuff in Dad's books are, too."

"So?"

She shrugged. "So, there's probably Wi-Fi."

It felt good seeing Justice joke about Santa and Wi-Fi, even if it meant I had to exist in a world where Santa was a creepy spirit who punished 'naughty' people with actual torture instead of coal in their stockings.

Lorrie arrived with two coffees and a plate with creamers stacked into a pyramid. "Anything else I can get ya'll?"

"Wi-Fi?" Justice smiled.

A line appeared on Lorrie's forehead. "I'm no good with it. Hold on." She turned around and shouted, "Judd? Come help these young ladies with their Wi-Fi."

The guy I'd seen monologuing like Hamlet pushed through the swinging door. Sorta cute in that nerdy-best-friend-in-an-'80s-movie way. Dressed in a highlighter-yellow tank top under a Hawaiian shirt, cut-off jean shorts, and flip-flops. "I told you I'd write down the password for you, Lore."

She waved him off.

Judd, apparently Keeper of the Wi-Fi, sauntered over to our table, pushed in next to Justice without even so much as a 'Hi, how are ya?' and held out his hand. Justice eyed him. "It's a weird French word. Easier if I just type it in."

Justice handed over her phone but watched cautiously. I poured three creamers into my piping-hot coffee and didn't wait for it to cool off before taking a big gulp.

The kitchen door swung again, manifesting a similarly dressed guy with dark, smooth skin. *He* looked like an underwear model. "Mamma wrote it on the inside of your order pad," the guy said in a French accent so cliche it belonged in a Lifetime movie. He held a camera in one hand and a slice of greasy bacon in the other.

"I don't use that thing," she told the underwear model.

He smiled brightly at her and then devoured the piece of bacon.

Judd rolled his eyes. "Excuse Bernard's fake-ass accent. He recently did a 23andMe and found out he's like 100% French. It went to his head."

Bernard made his way to my side of the booth and inserted himself much the same way Judd had. These dudes needed a class on personal space. "He is simply jealous. Aren't you, *mon ami?*"

"Ber, shut up." Judd finished and handed the phone back to Justice, then held his hand out for mine. I passed it over and watched as he entered the password and handed the phone back.

"Thanks."

"No sweat. If you need anything else, we'll be filming in the parking lot." Judd got up. Bernard took the hint and followed him.

When they were out of earshot, Justice asked, "Filming?"

"They've got a YouTube channel," Lorrie chewed her bottom lip, "It's popular, I think. They're always in the woods. Ridiculous, if you ask me. They're more likely to run into a wolf than a werewolf."

"They hunt werewolves?" Justice looked at me as if trying to beam a thought directly into my mind.

And even though that didn't technically work, I got the message. Rougarous were often mistaken for werewolves. A fact drilled into my memory courtesy of Dad's endless lectures. These weird dudes might know where we could find L.B., bringing us one step closer to the Rougarou. Maybe we could find L.B. before Dad caught up with us— just maybe.

"That. Other things." Lorrie placed a hand on her hip, settling in to tell a story. "They were convinced that one preacher visiting town was actually a vampire king. They stalked the poor fella trying to catch him turning into a bat. Judd even followed him into a bathroom to see if he had a reflection. Turns out he was just creepy and really pale. Mo, that's Bernard's mom, she runs this place—well, she had to give the preacher free breakfast for a week to keep him from filing charges."

Justice scrunched her brows together, forming a plan, no doubt, and subtly asked, "Oh, cool. Do they know other people who investigate this sort of thing?"

"Call themselves paranormal investigators. I'll be darned if I can remember the actual name of their show, though. Some kind of pun. Anyways, let me know if I can get ya anything else." Lorrie left it at that and sauntered back toward the kitchen.

Hopefully, the next time I saw her, she'd be holding pancakes.

"*Prue*," Justice said, fork halfway to her mouth. She'd been gawping at me for the last minute while I ate.

I shoved a particularly loaded forkful in my mouth, letting some excess Nutella drip on my chin because I knew it would drive my sister crazy. I watched her eyes dart to the napkin she so clearly wanted to offer me.

"I Googled them," she said.

"And?"

She flipped her phone around. Their page had over a hundred thousand subscribers. Not bad, but certainly not famous. My eyes scanned their most recent videos and landed on one labeled: *The Unsettling Myth of the Rougarou of Louisiana.*

I pointed and mumbled, "Look, they have a Rougarou one," but since I'd shoved another bite of pancakes in my mouth, it sounded like gibberish.

"Yeah, we should talk to them," Justice said, not bothering to ask me to close my mouth. "I doubt they have any real evidence, but we should check. Everything is a lead right now."

"You're still on board?" I asked, swallowing hard around the pancake. "If the cop told Dad where we are…"

"Look, I say we keep going. If anything, we will have solid leads for Dad, right?" Gone was the Justice who'd had an '07 Brittany meltdown in the car. In her place stood get-every-question-on-a-pop-quiz-right Justice.

I didn't want to say what I was thinking, which was, "hell will freeze over before I let Dad help me," so instead, I said, "Solid leads are a must."

"One way or another, we will make sure Mom's killer is brought to justice."

"One way or the other?" I asked, feeling a jolt of adrenaline quicken my heartbeat, "there's only one way for this to end. We kill it."

Justice fiddled with the collar of her shirt and looked like she was fighting indigestion. "I sort of thought maybe we could find another way that doesn't involve," she paused, shifting into a whisper-yell, "murdering an innocent person."

"They're not innocent." It's what I'd told myself since we left the house. They couldn't be innocent because I'd be a murderer if they were. If they were as guilty as the Rougarou, then I was avenging my mom.

"Prue, we don't know that for sure. There isn't a lot of lore about it because most people who're cursed don't live long enough to tell anyone. Like are they conscious but unable to take control or their bodies? Or is it more like they blackout for the duration?"

"Or maybe they're just monsters, too, and they're conscious the whole time. That's equally as possible, right?"

Justice sat up straighter and rubbed the back of her neck. "Yes, but..."

"But nothing. We agreed to end this, and so we will."

"In Dad's manuscript, there was a mention of separating the curse from the person, so shouldn't we at least see if that's possible first?"

"It said it failed."

"Let's ask L.B. when we find them."

"Shh," I hissed through my teeth when I saw Hoyt come out of the kitchen. She had a motel key in hand.

"Mo said you can pay her in the morning." Hoyt dropped the key on the table. Under the bright lights, she looked exhausted. Her fierce, predatory eyes were bloodshot and red-rimmed, and it seemed like a permanent worry line had etched itself between her furrowed brow. "Do me a favor, don't drive 'til it's light. That... the car thief is still out there, and he's dangerous. Understood?"

I tilted my head to look up at Hoyt. Something in her tone worried me. On the surface, her orders sounded like just that, but something else lingered. She sounded afraid....

"We're tired anyway," Justice told her.

Hoyt nodded once and moved to leave.

"Did—uh, did you report that you found the car?" I asked, desperate to know how long we had before Dad descended on us.

Hoyt's stern gaze landed on me. "No. I'm not even sure how he managed to report it stolen when it's not in his name."

"Yeah, weird." Dad had friends on the force, that's how.

"We've got service now," Justice held her phone up. "I'll call him and let him know we're okay."

Hoyt worked her mouth into something akin to a smile. "And remind him that creating false reports is illegal, won't you? I get that a parent worries, but still."

Before we could say anything, the walkie clipped to her belt crackled to life. "Officer Hoyt, do you read?" The sheriff's voice sounded just as all-American as before, only a bit more serious.

"Copy. Status?" Hoyt returned, giving Justice a polite nod as if to say, 'police business, one moment.' No response. Hoyt half-turned away from our table and said, "You there?"

"Char, get to Seven Bridges. I found… car thief… he's…" the walkie cut out, and Hoyt grabbed the receiver on her shoulder. "Sheriff, do you copy?" Silence. Hoyt started down at the silent walkie. "Do you copy?"

Lorrie came over to our table, red lips parted into a soft smile. "Can I get you anything, Charline?"

Hoyt jerked at the sound of Lorrie's approach. She seemed to realize everyone was watching her and clipped her walkie back in place just as her stoic, everything-is-fine face manifested. "I've got to get back out on patrol."

"Thank you again," Justice told Hoyt as the cop turned to leave. Hoyt nodded at her and headed to the door with a noticeable pep in her step that looked like a nervous fast walk if I didn't know better.

Lorrie held up a coffee pot. "More?"

I groaned as I slid my empty mug across the table. "God, yes." I felt practically giddy with relief. Hoyt hadn't told Dad. We had time. We could still do this.

Lorrie's smile widened at me as she poured. She had a chip in her front tooth that added to her charm. "I've never seen anyone enjoy pancakes and coffee as much as you, darlin'."

Before anyone else could comment on my eating habits, a shriek ripped through the white noise of the diner. No one but Justice and I seemed to care. We both peered out the window near our booth, trying to find the source.

"Don't pay that any mind," Lorrie said like she regularly heard shrieks of bloody murder.

I glanced at her, wondering how serious she was, and saw her roll her eyes. I settled back in the booth. "And why shouldn't we?"

Justice sat down but looked ready to jump to action if she didn't like Lorrie's answer—and the dark part of my brain chided, "see, if Justice had been at home, she wouldn't have frozen. Look at her, poised to save strangers, and I couldn't even help my own mom." I bit the inside of my cheek, using the pain to keep me from spiraling down into my own Shame Oubliette.

"Sometimes they like to do their own sound effects. More authentic. Judd's actually getting better. He used to sound like a dying cat. Now, he sounds like a person getting mauled by a cat. Neat, huh?"

Justice eyed Lorrie. "You mean this happens *regularly*?"

"Mo originally begged them not to, but Bernard claims there's nowhere as 'aesthetically creepy' as the stretch of woods behind the diner." She jerked a finger at the kitchen. "Don't tell her I said so, but Mo's a big old softy when it comes to her kid, so we all just got used to it."

I was halfway to asking what the actual fuck this town was when Justice asked, "You think they'd let us watch them?"

Another red-lipped grin spread across the waitress's face. "They'd probably be delighted."

"Awesome," my sister said, and I knew I wasn't going to get to finish my coffee before stepping out into the humid night to watch two YouTubers scream through the woods.

Outside, Justice nodded for me to unlock the car. She ducked into the back seat and came up with another Morton's salt canister.

"What am I supposed to do," I took the salt, feeling both ridiculous and safe, "carry it like a clutch?"

"Frankly, yes." She looked at me like I was a moron. "Up until now, we've been relatively safe using the scent countermeasures, but this town with all the ley lines and, in case you forgot, the history of 'rabid animal' attacks," she pinched the bridge of her nose, "…just carry it."

My mouth went bone dry hearing the annoyance lurking in her suggestion. Old resentment slipped its way past the logical part of my brain that said Justice only meant to help; it settled in my shoulders, the betrayal I felt when we were kids and Justice sucked up to Dad during his games, even when she claimed she had my back, even when she agreed his quizzes were getting to be too much.

"Sure thing, boss," I said, using a carefully controlled tone.

Justice eyed me with a pinched, tension-filled glare. A moment passed between us, heavy with unspoken frustration, and I worried she might give up on me, on this insane idea, but the moment passed.

In one fluid motion, Justice scrubbed her free hand over her face and headed toward our best chance at a lead. Judd and Bernard had set up around the side of the diner. Bernard held the camera up to Judd's face as he perched atop a gnarled tree trunk and monologued. Neither turned around when our footsteps crunched on the lot's gravel. Completely absorbed in his story, Judd reminded me of someone on a reality show doing those confessionals. He thrashed his arms about. All bony elbows and rakish grins as he laid it out for the camera.

"Is this the best idea?" I asked, still wildly unsure that I wanted help from them. Bad enough that we had Dad on our trail, but now we were supposed to trust these dudes?

At that, Justice turned to face me and pointed her salt canister at me. "Hey, you're welcome to wander around this fucking town hoping to find one random clue that might lead us to the only person who can help us." She huffed out a breath that bordered on a growl. "It wasn't my idea to do this without Dad, without a plan. Okay? So, yeah, I'm going to take whatever help we can get, even if it is these nerds."

"Justice, I…" But what was there to say? She was right.

I'd been the one who dragged us out here, underprepared, to hunt down a ravenous beast with barely a ramshackle plan. All I'd seen in front of me was a way to make up for being a coward. I couldn't let myself consider any alternatives. For me, finding that thing and ending it was a plan. It was the only plan. I needed to draw clear lines in the sand: monster versus human. That was the only way I could make things right. Or at least not so fucking wrong.

"I told you that I'm with you," Justice said, "and I am, but I want you, for one second, to slow down and really think about what it is we're doing. If we kill them, aren't we doing the wrong thing?"

"Dad does it. If you think it's so wrong, why give him a pass?"

She dragged her free hand through her hair, dislodging the quick bun she'd worn the whole drive. "I didn't give him a pass, Prue."

I fought the urge to yell at her about how she absolutely had given Dad a pass, when another shrill yell interrupted me. The scream itself sounded ridiculous, but I still jumped. My heart banged against my ribs. I swallowed hard and saw that my sister had been similarly affected.

"Jesus," Justice said after taking a moment to breathe, then she gave me a weak half-smile. "Sorry, I didn't mean to, you know."

"I know," I told her, avoiding eye contact in favor of peeling the sticker off the opening to the salt canister. Again, we'd only had half an argument, momentarily dispelled by the task at hand, but I had no doubt we'd pick up where we left off.

"So how much are we telling them?" I asked.

"All of it?"

"For real?"

"You have a better plan?"

"Nope."

She gave me a look that said, *Well then.*

And that was that.

"So, in the dead of night, the Witch of the Whispering Wood pulls herself together out of the mist over the swamps and marshes," Judd said, billowing his arms out to imitate gathering fog and added, "Dripping hot, black ichor, she searches for lost souls who wander alone, whispering sweet nothings in their ear until she…"

That's when Judd noticed us.

"Mon cher, what the actual hell?" Bernard whined, dropping the camera to his side and slumping. "That was a great take."

Judd pointed. "We've got an audience."

Whirling around like a mad-tornado, Bernard's eyes widened when he recognized us. "Oh, how lovely." Fake accent back in place. "Can we help you?"

"We heard you're paranormal investigators," Justice started, affecting the voice she usually reserved for flirting with the cashiers at Coldstone when she didn't want to pay extra for the gummy worms.

"You heard right," Judd told us, puffing out his chest. "Have you seen our show?"

"No," she said, sounding pathetically earnest. "But we are interested in all that stuff."

"Yeah?"

"Especially the Rougarou."

Judd, to his credit, didn't immediately melt into a puddle at my sister's feet. His mouth spread into a lazy grin as he brandished his hands like the ringleader in a big top circus. "You just happen to be standing in literal Rougarou territory. Welcome to Seville, the home of The Wolf Man of the Swamp."

Clearly less eager to impress, Bernard placed a hand on his friend's shoulder. "Cher, they know this already, non?" The last part he directed at Justice, who smiled coyly.

"We actually came here because of the lore surrounding the town."

Judd cocked his head to the side. "That makes sense." Then he pointed to the salt. "For protection? Smart."

"I Googled it," she shrugged, "Actually, we'd love to hear about the Rougarou from experts. Everything we know is from the internet. Have you ever seen one?"

"No," Judd said, eyeing his partner. They shared an imperceptible nod. "But yeah, we can totally give you the insider's scoop. Lived here our whole lives, and we've interviewed people who had... experiences. Meet here for breakfast tomorrow?" Before we could agree, a twig snapped, and Judd whirled around. "Oh, maybe it's a bunny or something. Ber, get the camera ready." Without waiting to see if Bernard listened, Judd took a few quiet steps. "I'll scare it, and we can get some B-roll of it running."

The wind picked up, blowing through the trees. Their branches groaned under the pressure. I waited for the sound of animals skittering, disturbed by the sudden gust, but nothing. I might not be Ms. Small Town USA, but even I knew there was no way a whole forest went quiet like that.

I had a moment to think: *I should at least hear some rustling, right?* before all the hairs on my arms stood up. The urge to bolt overwhelmed me as I watched the edge of the dark woods.

Yawning, Bernard lifted the camera. "After this, I'm calling it."

"Sleepy bitch," Judd said, poking his tongue out.

I tensed, gripping the salt hard enough that the cardboard gave. "Wait."

Judd and Bernard, precariously close to the forest's edge, turned as one. Judd squinted at me. "Why?"

"Come. Here," I said, trying to keep my voice steady as I peeled the remainder of the sticker off the canister's opening. Next to me, Justice followed my lead and opened her salt. She clenched her jaw, and even in the dark, I saw the pulsing vein in her forehead.

"You're being..." Judd started but trailed off when a low, rumbling growl came from directly behind him.

I pressed my finger to my lips, begging him to shut up, and beckoned them over with a slight twitch of my head. Without needing to be told, Justice crouched down and poured salt around us. Bernard looked down at the salt, and his eyes narrowed with confusion before snapping wide in understanding. I expected questions or denial, but he grabbed Judd by the shirt sleeve and pulled him forward without another word. I said a silent prayer that I didn't have to spend precious moments convincing them to stand inside a salt circle.

Each step they took felt eternal, never-ending—fucking excruciating.

Justice hadn't closed the circle yet. Thanks to their slow scuttle, they were only halfway to us when another, more intense, growl came. This time sounding as if someone had ripped open the earth's molten core and let out a primordial monstrosity.

Judd yelped and slapped a palm over his lips.

"*Hurry,*" I mouthed.

I experienced everything as separate moments. Just like when Mom died. Just like when I froze and did nothing. Except this time, I did *something*: I clenched a salt canister. Sweat gathered on my skin like a morning fog, and I choked on every... stupid... breath.

Judd and Bernard ran, crashing into me hard enough that we tumbled to the ground. My grip on the salt loosened as we became a tangle of limbs. We'd landed mostly inside the circle, but some of the salt had been disturbed during our fall. Justice scrambled to fix it as the Rougarou lunged.

An insidious, overwhelming sensation of guilt flooded me. Here I was again, fucking up. Mom died because I froze, and now we were going to die because my fear strangled me until it was impossible to think, let alone move. My limbs were heavy and sluggish, moving like they'd been encased in a gelatin mold. Each heartbeat seemed to punctuate the beast as it closed in. Step. Beat. Step. Beat. Step. Beat. I thought about every Final Girl in every slasher flick and what they must have thought the first time they came face-to-face with their monsters. Only, they were facing some guy in a blue jumpsuit with ping-pong balls sewn onto it, and I was facing a literal Eldridge horror.

Justice shrieked when the Rougarou stood at its full height displaying the toned musculature of a Herculean god crossed with a titan. Thighs like tree trunks leading into a barrelesque chest, all culminating in a ferocious wolf face with all-too-human eyes, red and ruthless. And there, just above its knee, a nasty, half-healed wound. Yellow, blistered flesh. The fur around it matted with dried blood. A matching festering hole in its shoulder oozed pus as the beast flexed. Shotgun wounds. Dad had said he got it in the shoulder and leg, and that's exactly where this one had wounds.

I couldn't blink. I kept staring at the Rougarou, knowing it was the one that killed Mom. Knowing that somehow it found us despite all the countermeasures. I pressed my fists into my temples, willing myself to calm down. My gaze blurred and black spots floated in my field of vision. I pounded my fists against my head.

How the hell did I let this happen again?

That's when everything sped up.

I saw the bag of Lego in Justice's dropped messenger bag, and I remembered Dad sitting in front of a bonfire in our backyard. Dad telling us about the Rougarou. I'd been six and Justice four. We had our Lego with us, building a mismatched castle for our Polly Pocket dolls, when Dad reached out for a few loose bricks and said, "You know Rougarous can't count past twelve." I'd laughed and been so ecstatic when he scooped me into a hug. "That's silly. Everyone can count past twelve." And then, I showed him by counting out thirteen Lego bricks. It had been one of the last times I could remember enjoying those moments when he quizzed us.

That memory, the bricks—there was more to it, but I couldn't remember what, so in a desperate attempt to do *something*, I took the bag of Lego and ripped it open, tossing the bricks outside of the circle. They scattered at the Rougarou's feet.

"What the…" Judd said, getting cut off by an agitated howl as the beast eyed the Lego.

Holy shit! It's counting them, I thought as it stopped pursuing us and focused on the ground. The Rougarou dropped to all fours, snarling snout inches from the plastic bricks. Whatever the rest of that lesson had mentioned, I had no idea, but I hoped it didn't include a time limit. If the Rougarou kept focused on counting, we might get out of this alive.

Then the sound of sirens pulled my attention from the fixated Rougarou. A cop car skidded to a halt between the beast and us. Against the silence, the noise felt wrong somehow. Unnecessary.

With what looked like a great effort, the beast glanced at the new arrival. Down on its hands and knees, it could almost… *almost* be mistaken for a spectacularly large wolf.

The sheriff got out of his car and pulled a shotgun, which seemed as absurd as all the noise he made. The beast roared, saliva dripping down its canine jaw. The sheriff hardly flinched. He leveled the gun. Hands steady, finger on the trigger.

Nothing can prepare someone to hear a gunshot that close. Justice and I had been taught to use all kinds of firearms, but shooting on a range where there are safety goggles, earplugs, and the knowledge that you weren't in any danger made the whole experience surprisingly dull and routine.

Hearing a gunshot rip through a quiet night in a swamp faced by something that belonged in a nightmare, or at least a Guillermo del Toro movie, felt like being smacked upside the head with a cast iron skillet. My ears pulsed. Blood whooshed around my skull. I worried that I might never hear normally again. Another shot echoed, and the Rougarou unleashed an agonized yelp.

My head hurt, but I forced my eyes open in time to see its retreating form disappear into the woods.

"Great timing," Judd said, relief heavy in his voice. "Seriously. Great. Timing."

Bernard coughed, trying to gather himself. His palm splayed out over his chest. "I think I'm going to be sick." Then he doubled over and vomited right onto the salt circle.

"Shit, Ber," Judd said, rushing to his friend's side. He placed a hand on the small of Bernard's back and rubbed small circles while his friend heaved.

The sheriff turned and asked in a calm voice, "Everyone okay?" He hooked the shotgun in the crook of his elbow and surveyed the four of us. "No one needs a hospital?"

"We're fine," Justice spoke up. Her hair matted to her face, and sweat still dripped from her temples — the only real clue that she'd been scared.

I stood there, feeling... relief, marred by shame. I'd come to face down the beast that killed Mom and froze. *Again.* And I felt glad the sheriff showed up when he had because who knew how long the Lego distraction would have lasted. I still couldn't remember the rest of Dad's lecture on their inability to count. Hell, I don't even know if the part I'd remembered was right.

I took a deep breath and clasped my arms around my middle, desperately trying to keep myself from falling to my knees. "H-how did you know?"

I never got an answer because, in a hailstorm of kicked-up dirt and broken asphalt, another squad car skidded to a halt beside us. Hoyt eyed me as the driver's side window slowly inched down. "What happened?"

"Came up on these four staring down a wolf," the sheriff answered, hitting me with an everything-is-fine smile so fake it belonged in Stepford Wives. "Lucky, I happened by when I did."

"Did someone call 911?" I gestured to the car, where the lights oscillated blue and red.

Sheriff Rose turned to look, glancing over his shoulder at the woods where the Rougarou disappeared.

Hoyt, spared a brief moment to glance at me, squinted at the sheriff's car and answered for him. "We were in pursuit of the car thief."

"Right," Sheriff Rose agreed.

Hoyt frowned at him, jaw muscles twitching. To me, she said, "I don't suppose you get many wolves in St. Louis, but out here, there's all kinds of wildlife."

Resurgent anger hovered at the edges of my mind. Apparently, every adult on the planet was naive enough to buy that monstrosity as a wolf. Or, a suspicious part of my mind supplied, they thought we were naive enough.

"Lucky you were nearby, then," I said as casually as possible, giving them my version of a Stepford smile.

Hoyt brought a hand to the brim of her hat, nodding. "Lucky," she went on in a tone I'd expect from a kindergarten teacher telling the class that recess is over, "I think it's time y'all got indoors. We've got to get back out on patrol, don't we, sheriff?"

"Right, yes, of course… to find the car thief."

I looked sharply at Hoyt. "Hope they didn't get too far away."

Hoyt didn't look pleased, but in the brief time I'd been around her, I didn't think pleased was anywhere on her usual list of moods. "Bernard, tell your mamma that no one should go near the woods for a spell. I'm going to call up animal control in the meantime."

Bernard, still doubled over, held up a hand in agreement. "Will do."

"And maybe have her spread the word," Sheriff Rose added. "Your mamma sees more people in her diner than we can reasonably warn."

"We got you, sheriff," Judd said, slapping Bernard's back a little too roughly, causing a coughing, dry heaving fit.

"Hoyt, you stay here and keep an eye out… for the wolf. Least till animal control arrives." With a slight nod and another fake smile, the sheriff got back into his car and sped out of the lot.

Hoyt didn't move, but her hawkish gaze followed his squad car as he sped down the dark country lane. "Go on, get inside," she ordered. "I'll be here, just in case."

"Oh, my ever-loving fuck," Judd said through a shaky breath when we were far enough away from Hoyt and her open car window. "Ber, tell me you got that on camera. Like literally any —"

"Are you kidding me?" I cut him off and looked over my shoulder at Hoyt, who still eyed me seemingly with as much suspicion as I felt toward her. My first instinct got vetoed by the little voice in my head that sounded a bit too much like Justice. In lieu of a sneer, I nodded at Hoyt and returned my attention to Judd. "We could have died."

Judd shifted from foot to foot. "I… shit, you're right." He nodded but spread his hands out in a 'give me a break' gesture.

"But this kind of thing is unheard of. Actual footage. Of a… Rougarou."

"I thought you couldn't tell anyone or risk getting cursed?" Justice, the sole owner of the one functioning brain cell left in the group, reminded him.

"Well, yes, and no," Judd said. "If we knew the identity of the Rougarou and told someone, then we'd be cursed. But we don't know who it was, right? So telling people we saw one wouldn't curse us."

"We're pretty sure," Bernard added.

"Okay — wait, what?"

"There's conflicting lore, but like 85% of experts agree that you'd have to know the identity to be cursed."

"More like 90%." Judd grinned, which annoyed me more than it should have.

"Well, either way, we'll find out. Since we've all just talked about it."

"Damn, true," Judd acknowledged with a solemn sigh.

"On that cheery note…" Bernard picked up the camera and dusted off some salt and loose pavement, "I'm off to bed. And, yes, Judd, you can come home with me and look at the footage."

Judd beamed at his friend. "Cool." Turning to us, he said, "Breakfast tomorrow. On us. Well, on Bernard's mom. Around nine?"

Justice nodded for the both of us. "See you."

We watched them dart off to the front of the diner. Justice didn't say anything until we heard a car engine turn over.

"That was too close."

"I don't trust them."

"Who, the guys?"

"No… Hoyt and the sheriff."

"Why not? They saved us. Twice now."

"Too coincidental. They happened to be chasing a car thief and saw us. Twice?" I paced the sidewalk beside the diner. "Did you even hear another car on the road? Because I didn't, so how could they have been chasing them?"

Justice's face fell. "Well, adrenaline, you know? We were probably too occupied to have heard the car."

"But we heard the sirens."

"Yeah."

"So how did we not hear a car speeding past?"

Justice waved her hand between her head and mine. "I, well, I don't know, but they did help us."

"Is there even a car thief?"

"Don't be dramatic."

We stared at each other. The weak light from the diner caught on the golden flecks in my sister's eyes. She had that serious look on her face. The look that reminded me painfully of Mom.

"How about we sleep on it?" she asked.

"Sure," I agreed, deciding any further argument wouldn't get me anywhere. "I'll pull the car around." I knelt to grab the salt. Even the short walk to the car felt unsafe. I handed the motel key to Justice. I watched until she reached the L-shaped building, walked under the flickering lights to room four, and disappeared inside.

Hoyt, sitting in her squad car, watched me watch Justice. I felt her eyes on me, so I waved. A short, half-assed wave. The interior light from her laptop illuminated her face enough that I saw her expression harden before she waved back.

Exhaustion settled on my shoulders, then. It felt like I hadn't slept in weeks, but it had barely been two days since Mom died. I walked to the car, wishing things could be different. Wishing so hard that I made myself sick with the longing.

As soon as I got in the car, I cried. One of those body-shaking, stomach-lurching, snot-dripping-down-your-face kinds of cries. I expected it to be loud, for the sobs to fill the car, but it happened silently.

Chapter Three

Surprisingly, sleep had come the moment I hit the creaky bed, and I'd slept the heavy, empty sleep of the deprived until Justice woke me with her, frankly, annoying habit of blow-drying her hair after a shower. I laid in that uncomfortable motel bed while Justice flitted around the room behaving as if this were any old day and not the third day on this stupid planet without Mom.

My chest felt hollow at the thought. Three days. *How had it only been three days?* It seemed insane that time kept moving at the same pace it always had—that the sun still rose and set, and minutes turned into hours, hours into days.

And each day made way for another, all without her.

I scrubbed a hand over my face, begging my legs to carry me to the bathroom, doing my best to keep my tears silent. After a quick change into clean clothes and a splash of cold water on my face, I emerged to find Justice looking perky and awake and not at all like the unmoored zombie of a person that I certainly felt like.

"Too early," I said, yanking the hood of my sweatshirt up and pulling the strings until the fabric covered everything but my eyes and nose.

"You'd think, what with being an adult, you'd be used to getting up before noon."

"I'm barely an adult," I told her as we left the motel room. Moments ago, Justice's whole 'today is just a normal day' routine annoyed me, but at this moment, I felt grateful that we could slip into our usual banter. She tells me that I'm not a people person, or a morning person, or something, and then I hit her with my classic sarcastic wit.

She laughed amiably. "Good point."

I thought about keeping the banter up, but that took effort, so I simply groaned before adding, "Coffee."

"Coffee awaits." Justice dramatically gestured to the door and the diner beyond like she'd found the lost city of Atlantis.

I nodded. She had a point, and I needed the distraction.

Justice shoved me out the door. I groaned, which only solicited another shove. The rain fell in fat droplets that soaked my hood, but I couldn't bring myself to care. Justice, meanwhile, pulled an umbrella out of her messenger bag and, very Mary Poppins-like, strode off, not getting so much as one fat droplet on her perfectly blow-dried hair.

How the hell was she so together right now?

I flinched as we walked past the discarded salt circle, now a salt puddle. My sister, expert compartmentalizer that she was, ignored it and went straight for the Lego strewn on the asphalt. She didn't seem affected by the reminder of our almost getting mauled in a diner parking lot, which renewed my earlier annoyance.

"What are you doing?"

She knelt, keeping the umbrella steady with one hand, and picked up the Lego with her other. "I'm not leaving him out here." She threw the random bricks in the front pocket of her messenger bag but held Obi-wan up to her chest.

"Wow."

"What?"

"I just don't get it. Like you're standing in the spot where we almost died, and you're just, like, fine? Picking up Lego like nothing happened? Why aren't you a mess? Why aren't you more off balance?"

"I am, Prue."

"Really? This, this is you being a 'mess'? Perfect hair and a cute outfit?"

"You're, what," she scoffed, "you're mad at me for getting *dressed*?"

"No, well, maybe. I don't know." I bit the insides of my cheeks, trying to keep the nastier comments from slipping out— but the unkind part of me launched the attack. "I'm mad because you seem fine. You're perky even after sleeping on a lumpy mattress. You've been nice to everyone even though they could be lying to us. Shit, Justice, you're so put together, so unaffected, that I bet if you put a finger out, a bluebird would perch there and offer to braid your hair."

"And how should I be acting? Should I be *irritable*? Snapping at everyone who's trying to help me? Or, huh, I know… maybe I should plan a revenge killing even though I have no idea what it actually takes? Is that how I should act?"

Heat rushed to my cheeks. A lump lodged itself in my throat. "You didn't have to come."

"I was supposed to let you do this alone?"

"I could have…"

"For real? So, what? I'm supposed to let my big sister go on a suicide mission… alone… to avenge our mom? Sure, like that was ever an option."

I flashed a cold smirk. "And you call me dramatic?"

"You give Meryl a run for her money. Oscar noms get announced next week. Where should I send the flowers?"

I had two options: dig my heels in and make sure Justice got really mad at me, or fix it by skipping over the mushy 'sorry' stuff and barreling right into goofing off.

"Etu, Brute?" I took an exaggerated breath and clutched my chest, re-enacting being stabbed in the back. I got into it, dropping to my knees, regretting it the second my shorts-clad knees hit a warm puddle.

Justice rolled her eyes and stuck Obi-wan in the breast pocket of her button-up. "You really missed your calling."

I stood, brushed the mucky puddle water off my knees, and took a bow. "Thank you, thank you. I'll be here all week."

"I certainly hope not." Justice glanced at the woods, eyebrows kneading together. The Rougarou's massive body had flattened out some of the tall grass and crunched through a rotten log during its escape. If I didn't know what caused it, I might not even take note of the sodden path.

"Should we?" I asked, hoping Justice hadn't decided this was insane—or that I was insane. Seeing the Rougarou had both strengthened my desire to see my mother's killer suffer and reminded me how underprepared we actually were.

We both took a few steps forward, then stopped. "With the rain, our scents might be harder to track," Justice offered. Her knuckles turned white as she gripped the umbrella handle.

"Plus, our hourly dose of AXE."

"And there might be a clue?"

"Like?"

Justice grumbled, "I don't know. I've never tried to track a wolf-man before. Maybe a footprint? Something like that."

I took a tentative step brushing a rain droplet off the end of my nose. "Okay, so off we go?"

"Off we go."

"Why do I get the feeling that despite the threat of imminent danger, you want to sing 'Into the Woods' right now?"

Justice snorted in an unladylike fashion. The sound brought a choked laugh out of me, and we stood there on the edge of the swampy woods, laughing. The moment seemed to heal some of the nasty things we said to each other. We weren't okay, but we would get there.

"Mornin'," the sheriff said, appearing behind us holding a bright yellow umbrella overhead.

Justice and I both squealed and whirled around. My heart lodged firmly in my throat, and I noted Justice clutching her chest.

"Bit jumpy after everything," he said kindly. "It's lucky you weren't hurt." Sweat beaded his forehead, adding a sheen to his ghostly pallor that made him look moments away from heatstroke.

"Are you… okay?" I asked him, doing my best to keep from being grossed out by the excessive sweat stains under his arms. The tan uniform also showed sweat stains around the collar and above his waistline. Compared to the uniform he wore last night, this one fit snuggly, pinching his biceps and creating valleys in his skin.

"Fine, just fine." He took a white cloth out of his pants pocket and dabbed the sweat as it dripped down his temples, flashing a half-hearted smile. "Humidity will get ya every time, but I'm sure you know about that, being from St. Louis."

"Yeah, even when it rains, the humidity feels insane," Justice agreed, nodding to her own umbrella. "Sometimes I wet a rag in cold water and drape it over the back of my neck."

The sheriff inched forward, pulling at his tightly buttoned collar. He swayed like he'd just gotten off the Gravitron at the state fair…

I frowned and looked closer. Was that gauze under his collar?

Before I could get a better look, he straightened up, obscuring my view. "Mmm, maybe I should get a cold rag from Mo before heading out."

I glanced around the parking lot and saw we were alone, so I took a chance. "Uh, can I ask if you caught that car thief yet?"

To his credit, the sheriff didn't immediately tell me to mind my business, but he did check his watch, making an obvious show of it. He might as well have said, "well, look at the time," with all the subtlety of his gesture. "Don't you ladies worry about that thief. The real concern right now is the wolves."

"Were more spotted?" Justice asked.

"No, but that don't mean it ain't dangerous for y'all to be hanging about at the edge of the woods." He licked his lips and blew a heavy sigh.

"I mean, a car thief is still pretty scary. I'd feel better knowing you got them." I didn't do the doe-eyed thing as well as Justice, but it worked for me sometimes.

The sheriff nodded, touching the brim of his hat with his index finger. "Fair 'nough. I can tell you we apprehended someone early this morning, but that's it."

I tried that sister-mind-meld thing Justice was always using. I looked at her from my periphery and raised my eyebrows, hoping she understood my skepticism. *Could he have been any more vague?* My theory that there never had been a car thief started feeling more likely.

She responded by shooting me a confused glance. Guess my mind-meld skills needed work.

"We should get you two in… indoors before the rain gets much worse." He moved his free hand toward my shoulder but twitched it back before he made contact. "And I think I could use a cup of joe, myself."

"Are you *sure* you're okay?" I asked. His entire shirt now looked soaked through, turning it from a tan into a muddy brown color.

"Fine, just fine." His eyes darted from the woods to us, then to the diner. "I'm fit as a fiddle, but this damned heat is starting to get to me. Might need a good long sit down."

"We were about to go for breakfast. We'll walk with you," Justice offered while I scrambled my brain, trying to suss out an inconspicuous way to get another look at his collar.

Smiling, perky people occupied nearly every table, jovially eating their pancakes and downed coffee as if nothing could be better than sitting in a red vinyl booth at a roadside diner in Nowhereville, Louisiana. It irritated me. The unequivocal aliveness of the whole place. Not even the waitress balancing a tray full of breakfast platters with one hand and topping off coffees with the other seemed to be in a foul mood. In fact, she gave Lorrie a run for her money on the whole southern charm front.

The thought of coffee, bacon, and fresh pastries renewed my will to live long enough to wish the sheriff well after nonchalantly standing on tiptoe when I walked past him trying to glimpse down his shirt. Justice gave me a look that said, "WTF," so I shrugged and tried to casually nod at the sheriff, but she just rolled her eyes.

Justice made her way to Judd and Bernard, squished into one side of a booth, staring at a laptop.

"I think that's an orb," Judd said. He pointed to the screen with his pinky. He held a piece of toast between his index and thumb. "Definitely an orb."

"Could be a glare. Not like I was worrying about lighting as we *ran for our lives.*"

"Skeptic," Judd accused.

"Morning," Justice said before sliding into the booth.

Still occupied by our conversation with Sheriff Rose, I mumbled a greeting. I watched him shake out his umbrella, dab another layer of sweat off his brow, and sit next to Officer Hoyt. As soon as he joined her, I noticed her shoulders tense, and she whisper-shouted something at him that made him tense, too. *Wonder what that is all about?*

"Hey," Judd turned the laptop around, "what do you think—orb or glare?"

Justice squinted at the screen. "Uh, could be either?" She took a moment to offer me a side-eye glance.

"Is this footage from last night?" I asked, my attention firmly on Judd and his laptop, even though the thought of turning away from the sheriff made the spot between my shoulders itch.

Judd nodded. "Not much usable stuff, but right before the… attack… when I thought I heard the bunny, we caught this on camera."

I pulled the laptop close. The shot showed the woods—looking like nightmare fuel—all dark and full of shadowy secrets sliding between twisted tree roots and overgrown brush. In the corner of the frame, at average human height, I saw the orb in question.

"Looks like a glare."

Bernard smirked, leaned back in his seat, and spoke without his French accent. "That's what I've been telling him all morning."

"But what caused it then?" Judd's tone suggested they'd been through this line of questioning already.

"How am I to know?" French accent, thick and sweet as honey, added an air of hauteur to Bernard's answer. He ticked the list off on his fingers. "A bit of shiny trash collected by a crow, someone's hunting camera, a broken mirror—"

Judd grabbed the laptop and shut it with a huff. "You can believe whatever boring thing you want. It was an orb."

"Glare."

"We could check," Judd said. "If there's some kind of shiny thing in the woods, I'll drop it. If not, we post this and call it an orb."

Bernard threw his hands up in defeat. "Fine. But I'm not going out in the rain."

Lorrie appeared with two steaming mugs of coffee and a menu for Justice. "Figured you'd want another round of pancakes."

"Yes, but can I have blueberries and a side of bacon?"

"Absolutely. And for you?" Justice ordered a bagel with strawberry cream cheese and a bowl of oatmeal, and Lorrie took off for the kitchen.

Coffee finally in my possession, I felt more in control.

"I'm going to look while you guys wait," Judd said, shoving Bernard to get out of the booth. "And when I come back empty-handed, you'll all see. Team Orb!"

"Mon cher," Bernard chided, "really?"

"Yup." He flashed a quick smirk and bounded toward the door, narrowly avoiding a full-on collision with Lorrie. She chastised him, but there was nothing in her tone but loving exasperation.

Justice nudged me in the ribs, so I turned to her, and she nodded toward the door. I returned with a sharp shake of my head. No way in hell was I letting her traipse around the woods with Judd after what happened last night. Dude had no sense of self-preservation. She pursed her lips and narrowed her eyes, but since she was on the inside of the booth, she couldn't move without hopping over me.

"You good?" Bernard asked.

I'd honestly forgotten he was there as our silent argument played out.

"Someone should help Judd look," Justice said, nudging me again.

She wouldn't drop it. I knew that much. And I wouldn't feel good about letting her go, so before she could say anything else, I took a long gulp of my coffee and stood up. "I'll help." My sister looked ready to protest, but I added, "Maybe you can ask Bernard about locating our 'friend.' Text me when my pancakes get here."

"Oh, are you looking for someone?" Bernard asked, pulling Justice's attention away.

I didn't wait for a response. I decided to act before Justice could. I'd been the one who orchestrated this trip, so I should be the one taking risks.

On my way out, I glanced at Hoyt and Sheriff Rose. Their conversation seemed serious. She leaned in to whisper something that made the sheriff bang his fist on the counter. A few people gasped but otherwise ignored the rattle of silverware.

He turned, nose flaring, as I walked past. My heart thudded. Not a full-on adrenaline rush. More like my heart was preparing to go full tilt, *eventually*, and this was just the pre-show.

Forcing my lips into a polite smile, I kept walking. Hood back up, I was out the door before I could process exactly why I felt so skittish.

"Judd?" I called when I got to the edge of the woods. "You there?"

Judd popped up from behind a twisted oak that had grown sideways and wrapped itself around a nearby tree. "Hey, come to help?"

"Two sets of eyes are better than one."

"So true."

The rain hadn't slowed, but under cover of the trees, it wasn't so bad. An occasional break in the canopy allowed the rain to soak through my hood, but mostly I was shielded. The humidity, however, doubled. Not to mention the mosquitoes. Thankfully, they seemed as repelled by the AXE as the Rougarou, so I was left alone. Judd didn't fare as well.

"Bastards," he cursed after squashing a few on his forearm.

"So, you do this a lot?"

Judd knelt near a pile of brush, picking through it carefully. "Often enough. It started as a hobby, but I think it's what I want to do as a living."

"Aren't you scared?" I'd meant it as a casual question, but when the words came out, I realized I genuinely wanted to know. Because I was scared. Scared shitless. And here Judd was, throwing himself into the woods where a Rougarou roamed in search of proof that he'd seen a flippin' orb.

"I'd be stupid if I wasn't, but being scared is part of life. If I avoided everything that scared me, I'd never leave the house."

I had no reply, so I grunted in agreement and searched earnestly. A few minutes of companionable silence passed as we made our way through the brush. Each moment, I stayed acutely aware of my surroundings. I'd decided to help in haste and didn't grab any salt, so I said a silent prayer to whoever might be listening that Rougarous napped during the day.

My phone buzzed in my hoodie's front pocket. Justice texted a pancake emoji and then the vomit face emoji. I was about to tell Judd we should call it when I spotted a torn bit of fabric inside a fallen log. The bark had been smashed, and the earth around it was disturbed. I carefully reached inside and pulled out the stained, familiar tan scrap. It had a brass button hanging on a thin bit of thread. The stain looked rusty-brown and could have been dirt, but a quick sniff told me it was blood. And in the sodden earth, I spied a footprint. A booted footprint. A distinctly human footprint.

Judd threw up his hands. "Nothing. You?"

Without thinking, I shoved the torn fabric into my hoodie pocket, kicked some mud into the boot print, and stood. "Nope." He nodded, and we both headed back.

"So?" Bernard asked when we sat down.

"Nada." Judd laughed. "I'm calling it an Orb and posting it."

"Here," Bernard said, passing the laptop. "Post away." Judd's face lit up as he started his task, then Bernard added, "They want to meet Mamma Black."

I turned to Justice, who had on her lecture-face — *Dad's* lecture-face. My breath caught on the guilt I'd been ignoring since we left. When I woke up, I had fifteen missed calls, two voicemails, and a barrage of texts begging me to answer. Justice had twice as many. I ignored mine with the deft skill of the official family black sheep, but Justice spent time reading each message and listening to the voicemails while I'd gotten dressed. The whole time looking as sick as she had the first time we went on Splash Mountain.

We discovered that he'd drove all the way to Aunt Penny's when we didn't check in. He pried the truth from her. She'd texted that she tried to stall him, but he freaked out when she told him we'd never planned on going there and hadn't told her where we were actually headed. That's when he told her the truth, about Mom, about him… Her last text to me read: *Uncool, kid. Call me.*

Because I'm obviously a glutton for punishment, I looked at Aunt Penny's text again, ignoring the conversation. Justice laid everything out for Judd while Bernard nodded along, adding a detail here and there. She left out the part about Dad being a capital-H hunter but told them about Mom. About how I'd been there. Watched the whole gruesome thing. Judd actually welled up. Bernard asked about the Lego, and I filled everyone in on my half-formed memory.

"So, what you're saying," Judd linked his hands together and rested his chin on them, "is you came here to hunt down a Rougarou on purpose. And you're looking for someone who can locate a specific Rougarou to find the one who killed your mom. And it is almost certainly the one that attacked us last night? Because it has wounds in the same spots as the one your dad shot?"

Justice nodded. "Pretty much."

"Sorta," I said. "We figured you might know L.B. since you do spooky shit."

"Spooky shit?" Judd asked, putting on an air of mock indignation.

"Yeah, spooky shit. Paranormal stuff."

Bernard looked close to laughter at his friend's response but managed to hold himself together. "I told Justice about Mamma Black, and she thinks that's the person they're looking for."

"Where can we find her?" I asked.

"We'll take you. Just don't let her hear you call all this spooky shit… or you'll never even make it in the door."

The person in question, L.B. or Lorna "Mamma" Black, as Judd informed us, lived as a recluse. Figured. The one person we needed help from, and she didn't like people.

Seville was quiet as Judd drove down Main Street, past a high school/middle school combo, three separate football fields, and the police station tucked away between other shops. It reminded me of *Gilmore Girls*. All the town needed was a gazebo in the middle of the square to complete the Small-Town Charm vibes.

The windshield wipers on the beige Subaru whipped back and forth, working overtime against the sheets of rain. Rumbles of thunder and quick flashes of heat lightning filled me with dread and maybe a little doubt as Judd explained Mamma Black's reputation in Seville.

Her reputation as a witch.

Justice sat forward, peering through the middle of the front seats to talk with Judd and Bernard as we drove. She asked them more about their "relationship" with this reclusive witch, and they answered by playing a video on Bernard's phone about The Duppy, a Jamaican ghost whose head was turned the wrong way round. Apparently, Mamma Black had dealt with them in her travels (obviously pre-recluse) and provided an interview; however, her voice and face had been obscured.

I ignored it and watched rain slide down the windowpane, thinking about Dad. My mind flooded with unasked questions: *Were you scared the first time you hunted something? Did you enjoy it after a while? Hunting things. Killing them. Why couldn't you just stop?*

My mind, the treasonous bitch, insisted on playing Dad's advocate and supplied me with a list of reasons why — some he'd said, and others were my own.

My loudest thought shoved all others aside: Dad was never one to suffer an injustice. Even small ones. There was no way he could ignore a person in danger. No matter what. That's why he still hunted, even though it was dangerous for his family. That's why he stopped to help that woman.

For him, there was no other choice.

Sound familiar?

"Shut up," I mumbled to myself.

Justice looked at me.

I smiled but felt manic as my eyes watered. Stupid tears. Stupid thoughts about stupid Dads and their stupid secrets. Every time I thought about Dad losing his family, my righteous anger faltered. When I thought about how he lost everyone in one night. How he didn't have someone to lean on.

Then, I thought about doing this without Justice.

Without her comforting presence always just in reach. Not hunting the beast. *No.* Just life. Being alone in this. Completely alone. Losing Mom and having no one to lean on. No one to share a meaningful look with. No one to hold while you cried.

If I needed someone, I had Justice.

Dad didn't have that.

My hand clenched around my phone, my fingers itching to text Dad and throw the towel in, but then Judd announced we were almost there, pulling me out of my shame spiral.

"She lives sort of in a weird spot," he added, "Just a head's up."

"Weird, how?" I asked as Judd pulled off the main road onto a dirt road that no one would ever think to drive down unless they were trying to find the Cabin in the Woods cabin.

The car shook as the road shifted to mud-packed divots. I half-expected to see the Blair Witch peering out from behind the twisted vines and aberrant tree branches that wound together overhead into a coiled canopy.

"Like out-of-the-way recluse weird." Judd flicked on the high beams, and though it was still mid-morning, the marriage of the harrowing storm and the tree-canopy created a pseudo-nighttime.

"He's underselling it." Bernard twisted in his seat. "She lives in an abandoned church. In an old cemetery."

On any other day, I might have had a witty comeback or complained that Louisiana weather seemed downright biblical just to distract myself, but a crack of thunder rattled the car as the sky burned above us. The lightning strike's brightness penetrated the tree's cover. I jumped, clamping a hand down over Justice's. She squeezed back.

Oh, look at yourself. Lightning and thunder have you jumping out of your skin. How can you possibly face your mother's killer? Someone should have locked me in my room. This had to be the absolute most ridiculous thing I'd ever done. Justice could die. I could be responsible for her death. And my own.

Then Dad would be alone again.

And Mom would still be dead.

I let out a panicked chuckle and ran a hand over my face. No one seemed to notice my mini-meltdown, though. Everyone else's focus had been trained on the wrought-iron gate Judd drove through. When the gate creaked closed behind us, I shuddered.

This was stupid.

Judd and Bernard might be harmless, but Mamma Black could be dangerous. She could be pissed that we called on her. I didn't have time to tell Judd to turn around. He parked next to a crumbling stone church affixed with crawling vines and stained-glass windows with high arches and smoke coming out of a stove-pipe chimney tacked to the side of the building.

Judd turned the car off and opened his door. The pounding of the rain falling on sodden earth filled the car. "Let us go in first. Explain everything. We'll come to get you when it's okay." He and Bernard dashed up the stone steps, knocked on the massive wooden door, and disappeared inside.

"This is," Justice said, scanning the church, "well, it's just plain creepy. That's what it is."

"I'm sorry." I didn't know exactly why I said it or what I was apologizing for. The list was long and getting longer the more I dug my heels in.

"I'm sorry, too."

"What? Why?"

"Prue, come on." Justice faced me. "I know it's easier for me. With Dad. He's always gotten me, you know? We're both nerds. We can talk for hours about occult stuff. We're close. And, while I'm mad at him, I know I'll forgive him because he's my friend as well as my dad. I know he isn't that for you. Mom was. I'm sorry. I can't imagine how that feels."

My face grew unpleasantly hot as tears slid down my cheeks. I clamped my mouth shut, biting my lips to keep from letting out the strangled sob that had lodged itself in my throat.

Justice put her hand out, and I took it. "I get you, too, you know?"

"I know," I said, struggling with each word.

Justice squeezed my hand one more time and let go. "We're okay. But just in case," she said, abruptly perky, but I saw pain in the crinkle of her eyes as she hit me with more AXE spray and handed me a smaller container of salt. From the looks of it, she'd stolen the shaker from the diner that morning.

"You *borrow* this, too?" I gripped the saltshaker to my chest before depositing it in my hoodie's front pocket.

She chuckled. "Maybe."

"What else is in that TARDIS of a bag, huh?"

I'd been joking, but Justice pulled out Dad's machete.

"Have you had that the whole time?"

"Yeah, well, not in my bag, but yeah. I brought it. I know we were joking about it in the garage, but," she shrugged, "better safe than sorry."

"You're insane. I love it." I smiled for a moment then remembered I hadn't told her what I found in the woods. I slipped the fabric out just enough for Justice to see it.

"What is that?"

"Torn clothing."

Justice rolled her eyes. "Obviously. I mean, where did you get it?"

"Well, I found it near where the Rougarou showed up."

"It's stained."

"Blood. At least, I think."

"Did Judd see?"

"No."

Justice closed her eyes and tilted her head to the side. "If it was... well, that... things are feeling hinkier." My sister opened her eyes wide and said, "The fabric looks like the cop uniforms."

"I told you."

"Prue, be reasonable. How could it be them? We saw both of them *and* the Rougarou at the same time."

Right. "Well, maybe there's more than one?"

"And you think they could be one? And that they shot the other to what?"

"Throw us off their scent?"

"Really?"

"Okay, no. It sounded ridiculous even as I said it." I eyed the front of the church, wondering what was taking so long. "It was a cop uniform, though."

"Yeah."

"Okay, but did you notice how gross the sheriff looked?"

"Really, Prue?"

Now it was my turn to be the academic-minded one. I grabbed my phone, opened the photos app, and selected the page from Dad's book about what kinds of symptoms cursed humans experience.

I turned my phone to show her the section on symptoms. "Here, it says that cursed humans will appear sweaty, tired, and gross."

"It does not say 'gross.'"

"No, but it should because these symptoms sound gross."

"That's true, but..." She rolled her eyes. "He did look ill, I will say that, but it could just be the heat."

"Or it could be him. We need to end this, end it before Dad gets here."

"Before we do anything we can't undo, let's see this Mamma Black thing through. Be sure, you know?"

"Fine," I agreed, secretly happy that Justice had a logical reason why we shouldn't go after the sheriff right now. I didn't want to admit it, but ever since our encounter with the Rougarou...ever since I'd come close to letting that thing kill Justice just like I'd let it kill Mom... I was scared.

Whatever Judd had said to the recluse must have worked because he stood at the door waving at us. My sister made me promise to keep a level head before we got out and jogged over to Judd.

Chapter Four

"Okay, so she's agreed to meet you guys. Just, you know, be nice." Judd looked at me when he said that, then led us down the front hall of the church into an anteroom with a big oak table with newspapers and mail stacked in haphazard piles. On either side of the table stood two doors that led into the church proper.

Melting tapers in sconces lit the anteroom. The candlelight flickered, captured in mirrors of all shapes and sizes covering the walls. Some encased in bronze, others plated in gold. Most were wavy, like old glass, or had a tarnished look that gave the impression of looking in funhouse mirrors.

When Judd opened the door, I noticed most of the wooden pews remained in place. Books and bobbles covered most of them, while others looked to be used as drying racks for herbs and flowers. On a few lay throw pillows and cushions. A makeshift couch, probably.

At the front, where the preacher stood to give the sermon, sat a round table with a purple tablecloth draped over it. Melting candles sat at the center. I counted four empty chairs and one occupied by Bernard, who sipped something out of a porcelain teacup missing its handle.

"You guys want some lavender tea?" Bernard asked, but I didn't see a teapot. Just more half-cracked teacups and a mason jar.

"Where is it?" I asked.

"Mamma Black's bringing more."

Like her name had been a summoning spell, a woman holding a steaming kettle appeared from a doorway to the right of the raised altar. Tightly woven braids held her dark hair in place. She wore a multi-colored silk scarf tied in a knot around her throat. A pinkish-white scar peaked out from beneath. With a honeyed complexion, sharp cheekbones, and dark brown eyes, she could have been Bernard's older sister.

"You must be Prudence and Justice," Mamma Black said. Her timber held a hint of a New York accent but not enough to make her sound like one of the Sopranos. Just enough to tell me she wasn't from Seville.

"Hi, Miss Black. Thank you for meeting us." Justice extended a hand, but Mamma Black didn't take it, so Justice let her hand drop and cleared her throat. "Uh, anyway, Judd said he explained our situation to you?"

Mamma Black's lips pursed. "I'd like to hear it from you if you don't mind." She gestured to the empty chairs, and we all sat down. I ended up in the seat that had the most direct eye contact with our reclusive witch. Lucky me.

"Well, there's not much to it," Justice started. She accepted the cup of tea offered to her but didn't drink it. "We heard you can locate specific people, well, creatures, and we'd like you to locate one for us."

"And where did you hear this?"

"Sorry?"

"Who told you I could do that?"

"Does that matter?" I asked, getting a sharp look and a quick cut-it-out gesture from my sister.

Mamma Black looked at me then. A steady, unapologetic gaze. I felt exposed under her watchful eyes, like she read my mind. That thought made my chest hot as I tried to remember if witches could, in fact, do that. Nothing came except a memory of Dad showing us a cartoonish version of a witch with a warty nose and black hat. He explained that no witch would ever be so obvious. Most would be as ordinary as your next-door neighbor.

Pinned by Mamma Black's gaze, like a butterfly in a lepidopterist's net, I mused that no one would ever mistake her for ordinary.

"Why have you come here? Really?"

Judd nodded encouragingly at Justice. She took one deep breath and started, "Well, recently..."

Mamma Black held up a heavily be-ringed hand. "I want to hear *your* answer." She nodded toward me. "Why have you come?"

"Revenge." The answer came out quickly. The ferocity in my tone shocked even me. "I came for revenge."

"I see." Mamma Black sipped her tea.

"I want to find the Rougarou that killed my mom." All the rage I'd held coiled inside myself since blowing up at Dad escaped in one snap. My teeth ground together, and before I knew it, I shot to my feet. "I want to find that monster, and I want to kill it."

"Ah," she said, disappointment clear in her tone. "While I am truly sorry for your loss, my answer is no."

My expression twisted into an ugly scowl. "No? Just like that?"

"You may finish your tea and then see yourselves out," she said with a finality that reminded me of a window being nailed shut. "Judd, Bernard, it was nice to see you again. Tell your mamma thank you for the care basket last week."

She stood and exited the way she entered.

"What the hell?" I asked.

Judd's mouth hung open. He looked back and forth between me and the door. "So, that happened."

"I don't understand," Justice said. "Why won't she help?"

Bernard shrugged. "We told you, she's a recluse. I'm surprised she even met with you. When we told her your names, she agreed, but...."

"This is, well, I'm just..." Justice muttered, but I cut her off.

"Wait, she only agreed to meet us after you told her our names?"

Bernard nodded.

I shoved my chair back as I stood. It hit the wooden floor with a thud that echoed throughout the high-ceilinged room. She did know who we were, knew who our dad was—and refused to help.

"He got to her."

"Who got to her?" Bernard asked.

"Prue, come on," Justice said, but the line between her brows told me she wasn't as convinced as she wanted me to believe.

"Please, it wouldn't take a genius to figure it out. He knew we weren't with Aunt Penny…"

"Who are we talking about here?" Bernard asked again.

"Our dad," Justice answered.

Judd nodded. "Dads, man." He said it like it summed up everything about parents.

"I'm not letting him take this from me." I marched toward the door Mamma Black disappeared through.

"Prue, what are you doing?" Justice stood but made no move to join me. "She said no. It's over. Without her help, we'd just end up getting ourselves killed. Even with it, we could still die."

"It's not over." I pushed the door open with a loud slam. "It can't be."

I found Mamma Black in a small office at the end of the hall. She sat at an ironically modern desk looking at a MacBook Pro. The blue light from the screen highlighted her severe cheekbones.

"You're as stubborn as your father, I see." She didn't look up from her laptop.

"I'm nothing like him."

"How little you must know him, then."

"Excuse me?"

"The Everett I knew took great exception to the word no," she smiled, plainly amused by some distant memory of my father. "In fact, he abhorred it. I got this scar because he wouldn't accept it."

My stomach sank so far, so fast, I thought I might fall through the floor. "He… hurt you?"

She laughed then, a mad-barking sound. "No, goddess, no. He convinced me to help him hunt a vampire clan wreaking havoc in Savannah five years back. One of the blood-fuckers got me."

My eyes widened. A witch and a vampire? I wondered if the ludicrous amount of AXE spray would work like garlic. It managed to keep mosquitoes at bay, so I had hope. I leaned forward, bouncing on the balls of my feet.

For the first time since entering the church, I felt scared. I'd barged into a witch-vampire's office *alone*. Without thinking too hard, I pulled out the saltshaker, twisted off the metal cap, and tossed a handful of salt at Mamma Black, just in case. She didn't balk. Her skin didn't burn like acid like a Rougarou's would, thank God. I let out a breath I'd been holding in.

Brushing the salt off her face and chest, she laughed again, this time softer, kinder. "I'm not a cursed beast. Salt doesn't affect me. Plus, you can't become undead if you have witch blood. To them, I am arsenic. Quite handy when one needs to dispense with a coven of undead, which is why your father asked for my help."

"Oh, right," I whispered. Relief fluttered through my body. "Is that why you won't help? Because Dad got you hurt?"

"Have you ever killed anything?"

Her question threw me. I'd expected more resistance, but not this odd mixture of sympathy and exhaustion. I'd had a million answers ready about why she should help us even if my dad told her not to, but I had only one answer to that question: *No.*

"I thought not," she said when I didn't speak. "Killing, even for the noblest of reasons, poisons one's soul." I opened my mouth to retort, to tell her I could do it, but she held up a hand. "I am sure that right now, you're willing to give up everything to avenge your loss. I don't doubt your conviction. That determined set of the jaw and fire behind your eyes is a look with which I am well acquainted."

"I'm not him."

"No," she agreed. "If you find this beast. What then? You've never killed, and I'm sure you know that a Rougarou is human—albeit a cursed human, but human, nonetheless. They have no memory or control over the Rougarou's actions. Would you be willing to kill an innocent person to kill the beast?"

It's a question I'd tried to ignore up until that moment. Yes, I'd known that killing one meant killing the other, but I'd convinced myself that it didn't matter. Dad said they held onto some semblance of their humanity when they transformed, so I'd decided it meant they were guilty, too, and I told her as much.

"Rougarou have some human instincts, true, but not humanity. They experience no remorse, no emotion. Think of them like serial killers."

"So what? Are you saying just forget it? Let the murderer get away because the person might be innocent?"

"Maybe. It would certainly be the safer choice."

"No."

She threw up her hands. "If I don't help, you'll just do it anyway?"

"Yes."

"Ah, well, I promised to stall you, and I tried."

"I knew it. Dad called."

"He did," she confirmed. "After reporting the car stolen, he called me and said to expect visitors."

"And to keep us from hunting the Rougarou."

"Precisely."

"He's on his way, right?" I dreaded the answer, but I needed to know how long until Dad got here and forced me to stop.

She picked up her phone and checked the time. "He should be here in two hours, give or take. He does tend to drive like a banshee when he's scared, so possibly sooner."

Not for the first time in this exchange did I wonder exactly how well Mamma Black knew Dad. "Help us. Please. If he gets here before we find that thing, he won't let us stop it."

"And is that so bad?"

"I did nothing. Nothing. I just sat there and watched her die. Do you get that? I just watched. How could I do that? My mom protected me, and I did nothing. How am I supposed to live with myself? How? Tell me. Because I have no idea. Every moment since she died has been agony. All I know is that *monster* should suffer. I want it to suffer."

"Fine."

"Fine?"

"I will locate your Rougarou." She held up a hand to quiet me. "My one condition is this: you let me come and attempt to separate the human from the curse."

I pinched the bridge of my nose. Dad's entry had mentioned a failed attempt to separate the curse from the infected human. I told her as much, using the least colorful language I could manage, considering how badly I wanted to go *Wolf of Wall Street* on her. "I'm not going to let it get away."

Mamma Black cocked her head to the side, narrowing her eyes as if confused. She seemed to have an internal debate and spoke when she concluded. "If I fail, you can kill the beast. And I will help."

"Deal."

Justice drank tea while I poured a mixture of black and pink salt around Mamma Black in the shape of a pentagram.

Judd and Bernard declared themselves Official Chroniclers of the endeavor and pulled a camera and small microphone out. It was debated for ten minutes whether recording this was a good idea. In the end, Judd won, and everyone, including Mamma Black, relented if they promised to blur our faces out.

And so began the most agonizingly slow fifteen minutes of my life.

Between Judd's narration, which included saying everything we did seconds after we did it, and Mamma Black's detailed instructions, I was tempted to brave the storm and search for the Rougarou without a location spell.

"No, Prudence, the salt lines have to be exact. Seville sits on a nexus of ley lines. If there is even the smallest mistake, the innate magic will overwhelm me. I'm opening a small hole in the fabric of reality here."

"A small hole in what now?" I asked.

"Reality," she said. "It's not like on *Charmed*, okay? I can't just hold a crystal over a map and wait for it to land on the right spot. That's not how magic works."

"I didn't think that." Except, maybe I had.

At the very least, I hadn't expected the ritual to be so involved. We'd cleared a portion of the church floor. Big enough to fit Mamma Black and her "boiling cauldron," which, to my disappointment, was an electric kettle. She had me light three candles: black, white, and gold, and place them in a triangle around the kettle. Then she doused herself in Moon Water, or as I liked to call it: rainwater collected in a mason jar that sat out during the last full moon. Finally, she placed a few jagged quartz crystals at the five points of the salt pentagram I drew.

As a precaution, she'd ordered us to stand a few feet back and pour ourselves a glass of water each. I'd asked why and all she'd said was "because," so I poured out five glasses of water and set them at the edge of the table.

"When I start, it might seem… like a lot," she warned. "Some magic is dangerous, and what I'm doing falls in that category.

Just don't touch me. Or talk to me. Honestly, maybe don't look at me. If I get interrupted… well, best if I'm not disturbed. Okay?"

"Um," I said, dragging the word out as Justice said, "Understood."

As for our self-appointed documentarians, Bernard gave a silent thumbs up and crouched to get a close-up of the salt circle, and Judd agreed quickly before resuming narration. I tuned him out as best I could, but the part about "two grieving sisters seeking revenge" was hard to ignore. I shot him a nasty look, and he shrugged in apology.

Mamma Black turned to me. "You're sure?"

I nodded, not trusting myself to speak. In all honesty, I wasn't *sure*-sure. A disloyal part of me thought this would end badly and gave me the singularly unhelpful thought that Mom wouldn't want me doing this in her name. But when I told Justice about Mamma Black's condition, she'd practically jumped for joy hearing there might be a safer, less murdery way that this could play out.

"Okay, close the circle and step back," Mamma Black said, low.

"How accurate is this?" Justice asked.

"Very, if I do it right." Mamma Black shook out her shoulders. "The spell lets me see through the ley lines."

I scoffed. "That makes no sense."

"Magic isn't sense, Prudence," she told me. "It's *feeling*." She adjusted one of the crystals and took a deep breath. "Now, be quiet."

Every inch of me felt heavier the second Mamma Black began her incantation. The barometric pressure in the church dropped, pushing me down into the wooden floorboards. My fingers and toes tingled like I'd sat in one position too long. I saw the same shock I felt stamped on Justice's face, but Judd and Bernard seemed nonplussed. Not exactly unaffected, but acclimated. It was the difference between an experienced horseback rider and a novice.

Bernard moved slowly, capturing a sweeping shot of Mamma Black rubbing Moon Water on her hands before splaying them on her chest.

For some reason, Judd sat down directly in front of Mamma and didn't continue his narration. Instead, he pulled over a small wooden box that held a bronze bell.

"What is that for?" Justice asked, stealing the words out of my mouth.

"Precaution," was his cryptic answer.

Mamma Black's voice raised as she spoke her spell a second time. "Show me what I seek, lift the veil, connect me to the creature whose name I speak. Rougarou. Rougarou. Rougarou. I call you thrice."

There was a moment of insidious quiet that seemed to pulse out from the pentagram, searing itself in my skin, my molecules, my everything.

"Answer me through the lines. Show me where you reside. I call you thrice. Reveal to me your hiding place."

I watched, mesmerized, as Mamma Black's head snapped back, and her shoulders rolled with it so her chest pointed at the ceiling. Her braided hair rippled around her as if submerged underwater, and her stern expression turned slack. At that moment, my feet twitched, begging me to move. Something about the spell must have gone wrong. I must have messed up. Whatever was happening didn't look right.

But I couldn't move. The air around me, thick as cement, keep me locked in place. I looked to Justice for help, but she had her eyes transfixed on Mamma Black and the floor around her.

I felt more than saw lines of power spreading out in a spiderweb formation from the pentagram. A feeling like walking on a rope bridge came over me as Mamma Black shouted the spell once more.

Her face, expressionless. Her voice, hollow. Her body, rigid.

And then, it ended.

And I collapsed to my knees.

Justice staggered backward onto a pew, knocking off a stack of books as she did. The sound echoed, breaking the off-putting bubble of silence that had formed.

"Phew," Judd said, wiping sweat from his brow. The small bell tinkled as he moved. "That was trippier than last time. Glad I didn't need to use the bell to snap you out of it. I'm not sure I could've moved."

Bernard rolled his neck and set the camera on top of the pew nearest him. "I feel like someone threw me down the stairs. Twice."

"Water," Mamma Black rasped.

Frantically springing to my feet, I grabbed one of the pre-poured glasses and handed it to her, careful not to disturb the salt lines.

A dreadful minute passed as Mamma Black chugged her water and put out the candles with the tips of her index finger and thumb. She stood, flexed her body, and stepped carefully out of the pentagram.

"I know where the beast is," she said, then passed out.

I moved forward to catch her, but the motion made spots appear before my eyes. Blackness clouded my vision, and I felt my knees connect with the hardwood floor.

I had a memory, sudden and intense as a bolt of lightning, of Dad and his infectious laugh as he chased us through the backyard. A laugh I grew to hate as I aged because it reminded me of all the things he loved better than me: His stories. His travels. Being right. And Justice.

I'd been eleven the first time I decided Dad didn't care about me so much as he cared that I was smart, that I knew things and could recite them back to him without making a mistake. I remembered reciting the five minerals for protection against the supernatural and saying nickel instead of iron. I remembered his glacial gaze, made all the more cold by his intense black lashes and dark olive skin—no more laughter—and how he beamed when Justice corrected me.

I hated him at that moment.

A sound like a whisper penetrated the memory, getting louder and louder and louder. Suddenly, I heard Justice shouting at me, and the blackness dissolved. I blinked and felt her gripping my arms tight enough that I'd have bruises.

"Jesus, what's with the death grip?" I asked.

Justice blew out a shaky breath and pulled me into a hug. "Thank God," she whispered into my shoulder before shoving me away. "You fell to your knees. I called your name like fifty times. Judd threw water at you. You wouldn't move."

I looked down at my hoodie and realized she was right. "What the hell, man?"

"You were in full-on zombie mode," he told me.

I asked, "Where is she?" At the same time, Justice said, "Packing supplies."

"Supplies. Right."

"You missed it," Justice said. "When she woke up, she chugged two more glasses of water and a five-hour energy drink. That last part isn't normal after-spell care, but she said she needs the boost if she's going to attempt another big spell."

"Sure, that makes sense, but what do I know? Did I really just stand there?"

"Your eyes glossed over," Bernard told me. He gestured to his handheld camera. "I recorded it, if you want to see."

"Maybe later." The thought of watching myself relive those memories, the thoughts about Dad, well, I'd rather face down the Rougarou with only a bag of Lego.

Judd beamed at me, and the urge to smack the smile off his face resurfaced. "Meeting you two is the coolest thing that's happened to us since that vampire priest."

"You're insane," I told him, but he continued to beam.

Over the next several minutes, Mamma Black reemerged with two black duffle bags full of witch shit. I resisted the urge to scream at her to tell me where I could find the Rougarou.

The truth was that with each minute that passed, I thought of a hundred reasons why we shouldn't do this. Why it was asinine and ridiculous and selfish. And a hundred more reasons why it would be okay to stop. Why it would be understandable to walk away.

Yet, there remained one very loud, unrelenting reason why I had to see my plan through. I failed Mom. And I couldn't live with myself. Not without trying to make it right—or at least make it less wrong—by killing the beast who tore her away from us.

"So, where is it?" I asked.

Mamma Black shrugged her duffel onto her shoulder and said, "If I'm right, it's at the police station."

"What?" Justice asked, incredulity dripping from her voice. "But that means…"

I caught myself smirking. "I knew it."

Chapter Five

We took Judd's Subaru into town. Mamma Black squished in back with Justice and me. The rain had let up. A slight breeze pushed the humid air around, creating brief moments where breathing didn't feel like a chore. We were as prepared as we were going to be. I'd shoved my hoodie off and tossed it in the trunk. Justice Axe sprayed our ever-expanding group.

Finally, I tucked a saltshaker in my shorts pocket.

All I had to defend myself against a ravenous beast amounted to a seasoning and cologne. At least Justice had her messenger bag with the Legos and the machete. The bag she seemed to be intensely focused on. She had one hand inside, wrapped around the salt, I imagined. Or the machete. And I couldn't blame her. I wished I had a weapon that wasn't *salt*.

"No answer," Mamma Black said after her fifth call. "I called the Sheriff's cell and Hoyt's. Neither answered."

"You call Hannah?" Judd asked, barely stopping at the four-way stop. "She's on the front desk on weekend afternoons now."

Mamma Black nodded. "Bernard, ask your mamma if anyone's seen the sheriff since breakfast."

"On it," he said, pulling out his phone and texting.

While he did that, Mamma called Hannah, presumably, who also didn't answer. "Shit," she cursed abruptly. "We need to get there faster, Judd."

"Fully breaking the speed limit, Mamma B," he said as he careened around a bend in the road before we hit Main Street.

I closed my eyes. *Mom, I'm sorry I let you down, but I'm going to make it right*, I thought, forcing myself to focus on her, not the fact that I planned to kill something, some*one*.

"Hoyt's there," Bernard informed us. "Ma says she's acting weird. Asking for meat to lure the wolf out of the woods, but usually, animal control does that. Oh, and Ma said she's making biscuits and gravy for dinner, and you're all invited."

Everyone murmured a thanks to Bernard's mom without any real conviction. I didn't know about them, but I wondered if I'd ever get to try Mo's biscuits or if Dad would be attending a triple funeral.

"Think it's for the Rougarou?" Judd asked, then, as an afterthought, said, "If it's in the station, then she's got it trapped, right? Why feed the thing?"

"Show them," Justice said.

I knew what she meant, so I grabbed the torn bit of uniform and handed it to Mamma. She sighed at me. "When?"

"This morning. I found it near where we were attacked. The fabric was near a boot print."

"It would have helped—" Mamma started to say, but Judd and Bernard both aggressively shushed her. "What the hell?"

"If you say who it is, then you'll be cursed," Bernard told her.

"Who is the witch with two decades of experience hunting supernatural creatures here?"

"You."

"We all know who it is though, right?" Judd asked, peeking at us in the rear view. "Or at least we can all take a very educated guess."

I rolled my eyes at him, but it was Justice who spoke up. "Judd, since we don't know exactly what kind of talking about the identity of the Rougarou can trigger the curse—maybe shut up?"

"Agreed," Mamma Black chided as the police station came into view.

Judd parked haphazardly in front of the station, which occupied a storefront on Seville's Main Street. He narrowly missed dinging a parking meter dressed up in a knitted sleeve that covered the metal stand. On either side of the station, cars lined the street, but no one seemed eager to be in the drizzle. A few people sat under an awning at the cafe two storefronts down. They watched us curiously as we filed out of the Subaru, each looking frantic.

How could Hoyt keep the Rougarou so near other people? In the middle of town? Sure, she had a cell that she likely locked it in, but still. This is the kind of small town that had fresh flowers in planters hanging from their lampposts. The kind of place where people haven't seen much in the way of gruesome crimes.

A few cars drove past us, splashing puddles and setting my anxiety on edge. There were just so many people. How many could the Rougarou kill before someone stopped it?

"So, what now?" Judd asked, pulling a fishing-style hat on to combat the constant drizzle.

"Should we tell people to leave?" I asked.

Justice looked at me, her eyes wide and guilty. "I didn't think of that." She said it like she couldn't believe I'd been the one to suggest keeping others safe. I tried to ignore the sinking feeling her awe prompted. It made me wonder if she secretly blamed me for Mom. Thinking that felt like dunking my head into ice water.

If she *did* think that, what else did she think of me?

"No one will listen," Bernard said, forcing me to focus on him, not the swirling thoughts weighing my head down. "Two outsiders, a recluse, and the guys who traumatized a priest? Who'd ever believe us?"

"You're right," Mamma Black said. "That's why you and Judd are going to get Hoyt. Grab her before she gets here and tell her what we are attempting. She can get people to evacuate."

"But, uh," Judd looked from the station back to Mamma Black, "you sure? If you run into trouble during the spell, they don't know how to snap you out of it."

"I'll be fine." Mamma Black looked at Judd like she couldn't understand how such an odd kid could also be so caring. She touched his cheek with the gentleness of a mother. "Go. Get Hoyt. Don't let her interrupt the spell."

Judd chewed his bottom lip, looked back toward the station, and seemed to come to some internal conclusion. He grabbed Bernard by the front of his shirt and dragged him back to the Subaru.

With that settled, Mamma Black, Justice, and I waved at the cafegoers who had watched the whole thing play out like live theater. They waved back, lost interest in us, and picked up their coffees.

The police station's tinted windows and faded taupe façade looked foreboding in the gloom. I clocked one squad car parked in a reserved street spot. Again, I thought about the people. What if Hoyt didn't listen to Judd and Bernard? Would she hurt them or lock them in her car to keep them from stopping her as she tried to stop us?

I opened my mouth to voice my concerns, but Mamma Black handed her bags to us. Justice took one, hauling it up onto her shoulder. Her own messenger bag draped across her body.

My bag felt heavy—what did Mamma Black need that weighed so much?—so I gripped it in both hands, tripping on an uneven sidewalk as we moved in silent agreement toward the double doors and mirror-tinted windows.

Mamma Black pulled on the handle, but it rattled and stayed in place. "Locked."

"Maybe there's a key?" Justice suggested. "Like under a fake rock."

"This isn't someone's house. You think they'd be that foolish?" I countered with more edge in my voice than strictly necessary as unease snaked through me, insidious and creeping. "Why would a police station even ever be locked?"

"You have a better idea?" Ignoring my question, Justice matched my tone and raised me a disgusted glare.

I pointed to a potted plant resting peacefully on the ground in front of the store next to the station. "Smash the window."

"That's subtle."

"Better than trying to find a key that doesn't exist."

"So, you want to add breaking and entering to the list of shitty things we've done since this goddamned road trip from Hell began?"

"You didn't have to come!"

"Oh, my God. This again? Prue, you'd have gotten yourself killed without me. You barely remembered the counting thing, and you certainly didn't have the forethought to bring salt. I mean, Jesus, Prudence, you never listened to anything Dad taught us. If I let you go alone, I'd be going to your funeral, too."

Her words rang true—hell, I'd thought the same thing about a million times— but it stung all the same. Each accusation smashed into me as if she'd punched me in the gut. I gritted my teeth, ready to unleash another insult, one sure to be the nail in the coffin of our friendship, but Mamma Black interceded before I ruined things beyond repair.

"Prue's right. We need to do this fast. Every second wasted is a second closer to this going badly, but a potted plant isn't going to work. I'll pick the lock."

Justice turned away from me. "Fine."

I knew when this was over, my sister might hate me. Or at least, she might never trust me again. "Fine."

Mamma Black told us to shield her as she worked. It took thirty seconds, and then she pulled the door open and ushered us inside.

Inside, away from the rain, heat, and curious townspeople, Mamma Black relocked the door before we all took quiet steps through a waiting area filled with vinyl-covered chairs. A flag stand missing its flag added to the emptiness of the room. I patted the salt in my pocket, just to make sure it was still there. The whole place was too quiet. I moved toward the front desk with its glass partition and peered behind it. No one, nothing. Except an overturned rolling chair.

Justice gazed intently at the plaques and pictures on the wall. "Shouldn't we hear something?"

"Could the spell have been wrong?" I asked.

"It could, but it wasn't." Mamma Black moved with cat-like grace as she tip-toed around the front desk, appearing behind the partition. She hit a button that buzzed open the door beyond, where the cells and offices waited. The sound filled the room. I tensed, half-expecting the bell to call the Rougarou forward.

As we entered the back of the station, I heard quiet scratching. So muted I convinced myself I was hearing things due to being scared shitless. After hearing another scratch, I noticed Mamma Black angle her head toward the sound, and I knew it wasn't my imagination.

"What..." Justice started, but Mamma Black held her index finger up to her mouth. She inched closer to the sound, which came from the closed door across the open office. A bronze plate declared it to be an interview room. With one hand on the doorknob, Mamma motioned for us to place the bags down and get ready. Justice and I armed ourselves with machete and salt, respectively. Mamma, to her credit, did no more than raise one perfectly arched brow when she saw the weapon in Justice's grip.

Once the door opened, I threw salt without aiming like I'd done when I wanted to check Mamma wasn't a Rougarou. Justice held the machete aloft but lowered it when a muffled shout sounded. I looked past Mamma and saw a man prone on the floor, duct-taped and handcuffed to a metal chair. The man lay on his side, blonde hair matted to his forehead, a bandage over his left brow, and duct tape over his mouth, which explained the muffled cries.

"What the hell?" Justice asked, rushing to his assistance. "Why does Hoyt have someone duct-taped in the interview room?"

"Let's find out," Mamma said, ripping the tape off his mouth after righting the chair.

He gasped for air, took quick, deep breaths, and started blabbering so fast that none of us understood him.

"Dude, slow down," I told him.

"She's crazy, man."

Justice looked at him with concern. "Who?"

"That cop, man. She's nuts. Bonkers. She, like, went postal and tied me up. I don't even know why I'm here." He took a break from his rambling to breathe slowly. "Where is 'here,' by the way?"

"Police station," I answered dumbly.

"I meant the town. The crazy cop wouldn't tell me. I'm not a frequent visitor to my town's police station, but I know it doesn't look like this place."

"You're in Seville, Louisiana."

"Dude, what? *What*? Did that cop kidnap me?"

"You said you don't remember why you're here?" Justice asked. "What do you remember?"

"Being at work." He tilted his head to the side. "Uh, it's blurry, but I remember a lady asking me to check her oil. I work at a gas station. In Arkansas. That's where I'm from. Then after that, I woke up tied to this chair, listening to some dog going ape shit or something. Lots of growling. Speaking of, can we get me untied?"

My entire body seized. A gas station. In Arkansas. I looked at Justice, whose face turned ashen. We both knew who we were staring at: the man who'd carried the curse to our doorstep, the man who'd been the Rougarou when it killed Mom.

But he wasn't anymore. The fact that duct tape and handcuffs kept him locked up and the mess of salt I'd tossed at him had no effect meant he'd passed the curse on to someone else, someone who I suspected wore a tan uniform.

I stared at the man. *Murderer*, I thought, clenching my hand around the salt shaker. Mom's empty eyes would haunt me forever. Her limp body. All the blood. God, the blood. And this man had been there. He'd been the beast when it drank from Mom's throat. Him. It had been *him*!

My closed fist flew at the man of its own accord, connecting with his nose. A satisfying crunch of bone and a pulsing soreness in my knuckles combined into a blissful release.

"Is everyone in this town insane!" The man said as blood poured down his lips and chin, soaking his shirt collar. His eyes flicked to me. "What is your fucking problem?"

I shuddered, opening my mouth in a muted cry, and rounded up to hit him again, but shaking hands pulled me back.

Justice breathed out, "Prue, it's not his fault. *Shh*. Please. It's not his fault."

I struggled against her, fighting back tears. "But it was him, Justice. It was *him*." I bared my teeth, spitting out the words. "It was him."

"But it wasn't," she reminded me, hugging me tighter. "He doesn't remember. He doesn't remember." Then, with an abruptness that made everyone in the room glare at her in shock, Justice said, "Leave him."

"*What?*" the captive said.

"She's right. We have bigger things to worry about, and he's been safe here so far. We can untie him after the spell."

"The *spell?*" The man squealed. "What the hell is this place? First, some crazy cop locks me up shouting about curses, and now this? You'll be hearing from my lawyer! I will sue your ass!"

Replacing the tape over his mouth, Justice said, "Be back soon."

I pulled the interview room door closed behind me and followed Mamma Black and Justice.

"Where are the cells?" I whispered, wiping the back of my hand across my tear-stained face. A dull ache throbbed whenever I flexed my hand. None of us mentioned my mild freak out, but it hung in the air—thick as the humidity outside.

"Through here." Mamma Black pointed to a heavy metal door at the back of the office space. The entirety of the police station could fit inside a small one-bedroom house, but as we moved closer to the door, the space felt huge. Empty and vacuous. And larger than it should be. All the while still managing to make me feel claustrophobic.

"Get behind me," Mamma Black said. "Be ready with the salt in case the beast isn't in a cell."

Justice and I nodded and watched Mamma Black open the metal door, swinging it in to reveal a concrete room with two cells on opposite walls. One sat vacant. The other housed a massive wolf-man, hunched over spilled pen caps, paper clips, and erasers.

"That's one thing in our favor," Mamma Black whispered. Her forehead glistened under a layer of sweat. "Let's make quick work of this. Justice, keep an eye on the beast. Prue, in your bag, there's road salt. Lay a barrier in front of the cell and then make a circle and pentagram like you did back at my house. I'm going to prepare myself. Don't bother me while I do it."

With our assignments distributed, Mamma maneuvered herself into the far corner, the duffle Justice had carried at the witch's feet. She sat down, crisscross applesauce, and began digging around in her bag.

As I went about my assigned task, I felt like the unnamed narrator in *The Fall of the House of Usher*, unable, or unwilling, to look at the crumbling facade before me. Instead, I focused on it in snapshots, which felt safer somehow. I ripped the bag open. Kept my eyes on my trembling fingers as they tore at the perforated packaging. Glanced at the Rougarou's long, clawed hand as it pawed at a paper clip. Thought about that claw ripping into Mom's flesh. Then I looked away, doing my best impression of a person who was fine and not at all wanting to hide under a desk.

A deep breath and a reminder that this was what I wanted motivated me to tip the bag and pour it in a semi-straight, unbroken line in front of the cell. I noted an unsteady line of table salt that Hoyt must have poured. I made sure I didn't disturb it. Each grain of salt hit the ground like a gong.

I heard Mamma Black start humming and jumped.

Justice put a hand on my shoulder. "*It's okay*," she mouthed.

Words failed me, so I *hmm'd* and returned to my task, trying to reconcile what I knew and believed I knew about this beast. If my suspicions proved true, the beast had jumped hosts — killing the Rougarou would kill the sheriff. And he hadn't done anything. Heck, he'd *saved* us. I saw that now clearer than anything. He'd saved us, hunted the beast in the woods, and got cursed for his trouble.

I couldn't kill the Rougarou. Not when it meant killing the sheriff.

Pouring slowly to keep from missing a segment and rendering the whole barrier inert, I eyed the hunched back of the Rougarou. I forced myself to think of him as Sheriff Rose, not the beast. I separated them in my mind. Man and beast. Innocence and guilt.

The bones that poked through skin and fur created a spiked, segmented look. How could something so nightmarish exist? And how could people keep it secret from the rest of the world? Shouldn't we all know about the danger? People like Mom might still be alive if everyone knew how to fight them. Sheriff Rose might not be trapped in a cell.

I swallowed down the acerbic responses to those thoughts, tainted by my anger with Dad for lying, and remembered what Justice and Mamma Black had both asked me: could I kill the person to kill the beast?

No, I realized with a sudden wash of guilt.

"We need to help him," I said, surprising myself.

"We are," my sister assured me.

My shoulders ached from keeping steady, but I managed to finish the barrier and the salt circle for Mamma's spell without a single mistake.

"Ready," I whispered to Mamma Black. She'd stopped her humming and placed her candles around the pentagram.

"Now, remember, you will feel the ripples of the energy from the spell just like before. It may cause the Rougarou to, well, it might react. Don't do anything to break my concentration. With Judd gone, I'm leaving you in charge of the bell." She handed me the same bell from earlier. "Only ring it if I'm dying."

"How will I know if you're dying?" The bell felt cold in my clammy hands but reassuring.

"You'll know."

I didn't like the finality of her answer, but I nodded. What else was there to do?

Much like last time, I felt the spell's effect immediately. I angled myself so I could watch her and the Rougarou, still occupied with counting, and then let the energy Mamma created wash over me.

Semi-awareness wrapped around my mind like smoke, blurring the edges of my consciousness enough that the overwhelming fear that the Rougarou stood mere feet away from me evaporated. I knew that we were in the police station. I knew Mamma Black was in front of me. I knew Justice was there, machete in hand. I knew we were doing something important, really important. I knew I had a job to do. The brass bell in my hand anchored my body to this moment.

But those things started to feel separate from my mind. Like a picture someone cut me out of—it still existed, but I remained separate. Instead, my mind sank back into itself. My memories, a sinkhole, pulling me under. The more I struggled against them, the deeper I went.

Dad laughing as I chased him around the living room atop my witch's broom (an old mop that Mom fixed up with dried wildflowers and hemp).

Justice quizzing me with flashcards as we shared a bowl of popcorn. Her laugh like wind chimes in a spring breeze every time I impersonated Dad's lecture face.

Mom begging me to give Dad a hug goodbye as he left for yet another lecture series.

Mom stroking my hair as I lay in her lap because I never slept well when Dad was away.

Mom showing me how to press wildflowers between the pages of leather-bound journals to make bookmarks for Dad when he was in 'research mode.'

Mom… Mom…

Mom bleeding, begging me to run.

"NO!" I screamed, my throat constricting as the noise shot out of me. Beads of sweat dripped down my nose. My chest hurt where my heart thrashed against my ribs. There was a hand on my shoulder. I stared at it. *Who did that hand belong to?* I found myself wondering.

Then I heard a bell ringing.

It took me a moment to realize I'd been the one making all that noise. I felt the cool brass but couldn't stop myself from ringing it.

"Stop!" Judd's voice joined the ringing, but he hadn't been here—he'd been getting Hoyt, hadn't he?

Hoyt.

I stared at Judd. He stood in front of Mamma Black with his arms and legs akimbo. His ridiculous Hawaiian shirt flowed around him like a cape. Inside the circle, Mamma Black chanted, her voice a whisper, her power rippling around her. Bernard knelt over Justice, who seemed to be napping. Her body curled into a fetal position. Her machete on the floor next to her.

"Justice!" I tried to go to her, but the hand gripped me tighter. "Please," I whimpered, jaw muscles clenching under my skin. "My sister."

"No," came a firm voice. I ignored it, struggling. "Stay put!" *Hoyt.* She sounded like she was in my head. I swiveled to see that the hand gripping me belonged to her. I clawed at her brown skin, digging my nails in. "Stop that," she ordered, digging her fingers into me so hard there would be a bruise.

"She's okay, Prue. She passed out when Hoyt tried to grab Mamma," Bernard answered breathlessly. He shot daggers at Hoyt. "She almost broke the protection barrier. We told you it could kill her!"

"I don't know what you *think* you're doing, but I promise you…"

"We told you," Judd pleaded. "It's a spell to help the cursed person not die! Mamma is *helping*. We told you!"

I jerked forward, but Hoyt's grip tightened. "No, no one moves." She had her Glock out but lowered at her side. "Not until I figure out what's going on." She lifted her gun slightly, pointing at the salt circle. "No one move, okay?" She seemed less sure of herself. Leaving the command sounding more like a question.

"Let go of me," I shouted. I dropped the bell, and it let out a final ding as it hit the concrete floor.

That's when I remembered the Rougarou.

I glanced at it, sitting in the cage, quietly scraping one clawed hand along the concrete floor as it moved a pen cap. Its torso expanded and contracted as it took even breaths. The absolute composure made my stomach clench. Something about it defied the reality of the situation. The eye of a hurricane. Steady waters before a tidal wave. An empty, calm, undisturbed quiet. I almost wished it would growl or something other than watch the scene play out through semi-intelligent crimson eyes as if the outcome of our disagreement didn't matter all that much.

"What's your problem?" I screamed at Hoyt, doing everything I could to keep from locking eyes with the Rougarou. It wouldn't do me any good to think too hard about how it seemed to be patiently waiting for the right moment to pounce. Suddenly, I didn't care that Hoyt was a cop, or an adult, or anything. "You have this *monster* locked up like a dog who isn't good around company. This thing kills people, okay? It fucking killed my mom. You leave it here, in the middle of town! Are you insane? We're trying to save him, for fuck's sake."

"I'm not trying to protect *it*," she answered, casting a forlorn look at the caged animal. Her voice lowered to a whisper. "Wait, did you say 'him'?"

"Shush! Everyone shut up!" Judd, still in his defensive position, aggressively shook his head. "Don't say who it is."

Justice maneuvered herself into a seated position with Bernard's help. She spoke carefully, slowly. A hand went to her head, and she winced. "We know who you're protecting, and we're trying to help. If you'd just let us."

Relief came over me as Justice spoke. She was okay. I didn't get her killed. At least not yet. I wanted to hug her, but I couldn't move. This mess was my fault. Again. What was I thinking? How could I be so stupid? Justice shouldn't be here. She should be somewhere safe. Somewhere far from danger. Far from me.

Without any warning, two things happened before I could tell her as much.

The first: Mamma Black came out of her trance, muttered something about failing and needing blood, then collapsed.

And second: Dad rushed into the holding area with a shotgun aimed at the floor.

"Dad!" Justice cried, scrambling to her feet and rushing toward him. She stumbled a bit, her legs wobbling like a newborn foal's. Tears streamed down her cheeks, and I realized how much she'd been holding these last few days. Her body shook as she fell into his embrace. He hugged her, one-armed, not willing to put the shotgun down.

I noticed the salt—the line I poured in front of the cell, the one that covered Hoyt's smaller barrier—was broken.

"Dad!" I shouted, pointing at the Rougarou, who stood in the cage now. Filling every inch of it with its height and girth. Red eyes glistening with eagerness, it grabbed the iron bars and began to yank them apart. Its skin sizzled as it made contact with the iron, but the beast ignored the pain and stench of its burning flesh.

In one smooth motion, Dad swung Justice to stand behind him and lifted the shotgun.

Hoyt aimed her Glock at Dad.

Justice and Bernard helped Mamma to her feet.

And I scrambled across the floor and closed my hand around the machete Justice dropped.

"Put the weapon down," Hoyt shouted.

"You don't understand," I pleaded. "The salt."

"I won't let you kill him!" Hoyt positioned herself between Dad's shotgun and the Rougarou, her back to the animal that nearly had enough space between the bars to stick its head out and…

A whip-like *crack* burst through the concrete room as Dad shot the beast before it sank its salivating mouth around Hoyt's throat.

A loud, prolonged snarl stripped away any calm I felt like paint thinner. Every inch of me shook. My teeth rattled, my hands trembled, even my bones vibrated under the weight of the

Rougarou's anger as it frantically, if futilely, pawed at its face. Dad's shot had exploded across the beast's muzzle, cutting shallow pits into the Rougarou's skin, snout, eyes—giving us a breath of a moment to regroup.

Having ducked when she heard the shot, Hoyt recovered her senses long enough to scramble away from the cage. "I'm sorry," she told the Rougarou. "Dear God, I'm sorry."

"He doesn't understand," Dad told her. "He won't remember this."

"I know it's not him, not entirely, but he's my *friend*."

"Everett," Mamma Black said, her voice a nocturne in a minor chord. "Blood. Figured it out. We were missing its blood."

"Shit," Dad cursed, "Prue, machete. Now."

I made up my mind in the second between Mamma's revelation and Dad's order. This mess belonged to me. I'd failed Mom. Lied to Dad. Put Justice in danger. This town in danger. I needed to make it right.

"Keep aiming at it, Dad." I hefted the machete into position. "You're the best shot here. We need you in case this doesn't work."

Hoyt said, "I'm a good shot, too." She tried to hide her unease behind a thin-lipped grimace, but it didn't work.

"Like you'd take the shot if it came down to killing him or letting him kill me."

"Prudence Ann," Dad warned.

"What? It's true, and she knows it. And we're wasting time!" I pointed at the Rougarou, who howled as it dug salt from its wounds.

"That doesn't mean *you* need to do it," Justice called from behind Dad. She looked so young standing there, gripping the fabric of Dad's rain-soaked shirt like a lifeline.

"Dad, you need to be the one to shoot, if it comes to that, and Mamma needs to do the spell. We can't risk either of you getting hurt. And I don't trust *her*." I pointed at Hoyt with the tip of the machete. "So, I'll cut it. Now, watch my back, Dad."

"Prue, wait," Judd said, letting go of Mamma's arm, Bernard taking most of her weight now. He picked up a salt canister, one of the ones Justice gave him, and moved to stand next to me. "I'll have this ready to toss at it."

"You're seriously insane, you know that?"

He shrugged. "Once-in-a-lifetime experience."

"Dad. Ready?" I glanced at him, afraid to see the disappointment I'd grown to expect, but saw tears in his eyes. I looked away fast, unwilling to let him see my own bleary-eyed situation.

"Be careful," he said, "Slice it fast. We don't need much blood."

I nodded. This was it. I took small steps toward the cage where the iron bars were warped. The Rougarou scratched its wounds, yanking its fur out and digging at the salt chucks embedded across its face. A quiet sizzling reached my ears as I cautiously stationed myself at the edge of the disturbed salt barrier. The salt burned the Rougaru's cuts, causing a bubbling yellow foam to ooze from the wounds.

Slipping the tip of the machete between the bars, I angled myself away from the gap and took a steadying breath, closing my eyes tight. Mom's face flashed behind my lids. I could do this. I could save the sheriff. I could be brave. I could make things okay again.

I parried, shoving the tip of the machete at the meat of the beast's shoulder. The edge sliced into flesh.

Nothing happened for an endless second.

I didn't move, and neither did the Rougarou.

My hand tightened around the hilt. If I pushed a little more, shoved the blade in further, could it kill the Rougarou? *Should I just end this now,* I thought, *while everyone else is still intact?*

The choice lingered between me and the machete, but before I could choose—the Rougarou snapped out of whatever trance it'd been in and wrapped a clawed hand around the blade. My eyes widened, realization settling over my skin like a net, and my whole body jerked forward, pulled by the machete.

My head slammed into the bars, catching me over the left eye, and something wet slid down my face, blurring my vision. I dropped the machete at the same time the Rougarou tossed it aside.

"Prue!" Justice screamed.

"Prue," Dad echoed.

Dazed, I reached up to wipe the sticky, wetness out of my eye. I watched from behind blood-soaked lashes as the Rougarou came for me, reaching for me from between the bars with long, bony fingers.

Mom.

Then I felt the ground come up to meet me.

And nothing.

Sweet, Nutella-covered fluffy pancakes. All I could eat. Warm, black coffee. Heaven, if you asked me. I shoved a forkful into my mouth, aware of the sharp stab of pain every time I moved a facial muscle. I chewed through the pain, though. Anything for pancakes.

"Gross," Justice said, pulling one of those faces parents warned would 'get struck like that someday.'

I shot her one back but winced. My stitches pulled anytime I tried to emote. They also itched like hell.

"One more time," Mo, Bernard's mom, said from behind the diner counter. She was beautiful, like Bernard, in that runway-model-meets-ancient-goddess way. Stunning, even in one of those vintage dresses waitresses wore that cinched at the waist and always looked wrinkled.

"Mamma, do I have to?" Bernard whined.

From my spot at the end of the counter, I could see everyone lined up, sitting on their stools, drinking coffee, or picking at their plates. Justice next to me, with Dad next to her. They shared a plate of chili fries. It had to be the least healthy thing Justice ate the whole trip but defeating a Rougarou apparently calls for heartier food than oatmeal.

Further down the counter sat Judd, Bernard, and Mamma Black—all three taking turns explaining to Mo what surely sounded like the plot to an A24 flick and not at all like something that actually happened.

"Yes, again," Mo told him, absentmindedly refilling every one's coffee while she glared at her son. "Unless you want to be grounded until graduation, you will tell me every insane detail as many times as I ask."

Bernard whined but launched into the story again. This time, I only half-listened. I already knew the beginning, anyway.

My focus lay elsewhere, split between pancakes and the booth where Officer Hoyt and Sheriff Rose sat, huddled together, whispering. I knew what she must've been telling him. That it wasn't his fault. That no one got hurt, well, not irreversibly hurt. My cut would heal. Mamma's spell exhaustion would ease. The cuts that manifested on the sheriff's once jovial face would fade and soften with time.

All the physical scars would heal, but I didn't think he would ever forget what being cursed felt like.

Because apparently, 'the cursed' do remember some things. That much had been confirmed when the sheriff talked to the man Hoyt had stashed in the interview room. The moment Dad explained to the dude, Carl, what happened to him after that gas station in Arkansas, he'd thrown up. Understandably, he skipped town with promises to forget I'd sucker punched him.

In all my fury, I hadn't considered what it might feel like to learn you'd killed and drank someone's blood. Even hearing it wasn't *really* you couldn't wipe away the knowledge that it was your body, your mouth, your teeth. And while neither man remembered being a Rougarou, they remembered being somewhere that wasn't their body. Mamma Black said it had to be what she dubbed, The Middle Distance or some version of limbo.

Carl, though completely innocent of murder on the technicality that he'd been cursed at the time, apologized to Dad when he heard what happened to Mom. He left before I even woke up. I never got to say anything to him.

Because after the Rougarou knocked me out cold, they did the spell.

It worked.

And I missed it.

Justice said it looked like a painting being smeared in a storm. Like Mamma Black's words slowly rubbed away the Rougarou from reality. Judd's version, unsurprisingly, had more theatrics. To hear him tell it, he bravely reached for the machete the Rougarou tossed and got it to Mamma Black just in time for her to use her magic to bleach the curse out like a stubborn grass stain.

Whoever told the story. The ending remained the same.

"We tried to convince Hoyt that we were helping," Bernard paused, looking down the counter toward the booth where Hoyt and the sheriff sat, "that's what we were doing here. She wouldn't listen and bolted, so we had to chase her."

"I was like Paul Walker," Judd interjected. "Tokyo driftin' in the rain."

"That's not even the same movie... Paul Walker wasn't..." Bernard started, but one look at Judd's smirk and he rolled his eyes, "anyway, we chased her down, and when we all got to the station, we, like, did everything but jump on her back to keep her from interrupting the spell."

"That's when everything got messy," Judd added.

"Whatever you want to call it, we managed to get the spell working once Mamma B figured out we needed blood."

"It's obvious now that we're on the other side of it," she said, her voice harsh and gravely, "Isn't it, Everett?"

Dad shoved a chili fry in his mouth just as she asked the question. He spilled some on his chin and wiped it with the back of his hand. "Separating the blood separated the bodies. It has a certain poetry to it." He turned his attention to Justice and then myself. "Thanks for helping my girls, Lore."

I shoved a particularly hefty bite of pancake into my mouth. "I need some air," I said, mumbling around the half-chewed food.

Justice grabbed my arm and pulled me down so she could whisper, "Talk to him, please."

I looked over her head at Dad. He locked eyes with me, so I nodded toward the door—an invitation if he wanted—and headed outside just as Bernard got to the part in the story where I got my head smashed against the cell's iron bars.

Outside, the air felt cooler than it had the last few days. The downpour had stopped to reveal a purple-and-orange sunset. A soft breeze blew past, singing through the branches and dew-covered leaves, and birds trilled in the trees.

I made a show of taking deep breaths since I'd said I needed air. Really, I just couldn't listen to the story again. For Judd, Bernard, Mamma B, and maybe even the others—the story opened their worlds, expanded their knowledge, gave them new and amazing things to think about.

For me, it seemed more akin to yanking the mask off the Scooby Doo villain only to find an even scarier monster underneath… and this one didn't call me a meddling kid and shake its fist at me when I got the better of it. No, this one wanted to kill me.

"Prue," Dad's soft whisper came from the doorway.

I stood under the diner's red awning, leaning against the large glass window.

"I'm so glad you and your sister are safe. You have no idea."

"She told you where we were, right?" Dad's perfect timing, showing up at the exact right place, had bothered me. "Justice texted you while we were driving to the station."

"Yeah," he admitted.

I'd thought she had her hand wrapped around the machete, but it had been her phone. I'd be mad about it later, but for now, the fact that Justice texted him had saved all our lives.

"She was worried that you'd…"

"Die. Or become a murderer."

"Prudence…" He opened his mouth to say more but closed it with a snap when I smashed into him and wrapped my arms tight around his middle. He tensed for a second, then wrapped me in an embrace. I cried into his shirt, feeling my face grow slick with salty tears and snot.

Dad didn't say anything the whole time.

I cried until my head felt stuffed with cotton, then pulled away. "I'm still mad at you for lying. I don't know when I'll stop being mad."

"I know."

"But I'm also glad you're here."

"I love you, Prudence."

"I love you, too, Dad."

Jorie Rao is a Professor of English at SCC and obtained and MA in creative writing from Rowan University, and was the recipient of the Toni Libro Excellence in Writing award. Her obsession with cryptids and all things that go bump in the night inspired *Out for Blood*—and if she can ever stop reading other amazing novels, she might write another one!

artist's rendition of the Rougarou

ROUGAROU

(Also known as *Loup-Garou, Rugarou, Rugaru, Roux-ga-roux, Rugaroo, Beast of Gévaudan, Stragoi, Attakapa Wolf-Walker, or Werewolf*)

ORIGINS: Accounts of this wolf man have been shared as far back as medieval times. Some cite the origin as France, having migrated to North America among colonists or those banished to Quebec, the Caribbean, or the Cajun regions of the South, centralized to Louisiana. However, accounts have been cited outside these regions, as well.

An alternate source for this cryptid is rooted locally in the history of the Attakapa tribe, whose name means "man-eater" in Chocktaw and which has been associated with legends of "Wolf-Walkers" vicious shapeshifters very much similar to the tales of the Rougarou.

DESCRIPTION: By early accounts, a Rougarou ranges from six to eight feet tall, is very muscular, and can be a man, woman, or child. It has the body of a human and the head of a dog or a wolf, with glowing yellow or red eyes and very reclusive behavior. The extremities also take on a vaguely canine appearance, with long, sharp claws and, some say, only three toes.

As with most shapeshifter lore, the Rougarou possess supernatural strength, agility, and senses. They are said to be able to see clearly in the dark, hear their prey's heartbeat, and smell its faintest scent.

One characteristic of this affliction is an insatiable thirst for human blood and a hunger for raw flesh. The outcome is that regions beset by Rougarou experience high accounts of slaughtered animals, both domesticated and wildlife, drained of their blood and torn to shreds.

More modern reports describe an aggressive, snarling man/wolf hybrid with brown or black fur that will attack anyone entering the swamp, forest, or woods, shredding its victims' flesh from bone and devouring the remains. Variations in the lore include a full transformation to the animal form.

In some accounts, Rougarou are said to become creatures other than wolves, such as rabbits, dogs, pigs, alligators, cows, and even chickens. These other forms are generally white. In some regions, it is said the Rougarou can take on any of these forms completely, almost indistinguishable from the real thing, except for unusual coloring and odd behavior. However, one thing that always remains the same is the ravenous, blood-thirsty nature.

One way Rougarou differ from traditional werewolves is that they can change form at will rather than being dictated by the phases of the moon. They also regain intelligence and awareness.

Some say this affliction results from a curse cast by a witch or transferred by being bitten by a Rougarou or gazing into one's eyes. Some variants say that a witch will turn someone into a Rougarou by first turning into a wolf themselves. There are those who believe that the affliction passes on to another when the Rougarou draws, or drinks, human blood, and others who believe it is hereditary, passing down to the third child of each generation. Depending on the version of the legend, the curse is said to last for 101 days before it can be passed on, or it lasts a lifetime. One thing that all seem to agree upon is that the cursed becomes a ravenous beast at night and reverts to human during the day, usually weak and sickly.

Among the Catholic community, the curse is said to be brought down upon those who break the rules of Lent seven years in a row. Other legends state that the Rougarou will hunt down and kill those who do not follow the rules of Lent, feasting on the blood and flesh of sinners.

When the curse has passed on, the original host becomes human again, sickly and remaining quiet about their ordeal out of shame and the fear they will be killed as a monster. If the curse passes because the Rougarou has goaded a victim into drawing its blood, it immediately reverts to human and warns the one who broke the curse not to say anything about what happened for a year and a day, or the curse will pass on to them, and they will suffer the same fate.

WEAKNESSES: There are those who believe some become a Rougarou by choice, while others transform as the result of a curse. Some also believe the creature could be metaphysical, perhaps of an interdimensional or spiritual nature. Whatever its nature, it is important to remember the Rougarou is still human underneath and may or may not be deserving of the curse. Killing, while possible with silver weapons or decapitation, should be a last resort.

As with any lore, there are always ways to protect yourself against the beast or to defeat them. The Rougarou has both common and unique weaknesses. As with vampires, with whom the Rougarou has been associated, this shapeshifter has the inability to count beyond twelve but a compulsion to keep trying, so scattering more than twelve items before it will keep it occupied until dawn is nigh and it must flee into the swamp. Surprisingly, they are said to fear frogs, and the caw of a crow will frighten them away. Another weapon against the Rougarou is anything blessed or consecrated, such as holy water, the ashes of the previous year's palm frond, salt, or blessed communion wafers. Ritual prayers or a roaring fire are also said to keep the creature away.

Aside from these, it is said that the Romani, native medicine men, shaman, VooDoo, or HooDoo practitioners can use herbs or other means to lift the curse, and certain herbs such as wolfsbane, angelica root, rue, sage, bay leaves, and laurel can ward off the beast, but only if gathered under a waxing moon. Some in the region carry mojo bags or folded leaves of wolfsbane in their wallets.

According to lore, a silver bullet or forged blade through the heart or used to decapitate is said to kill a Rougarou, or an alloy with high silver content, but the bullet or blade must not be removed from the wound or the Rougarou with regenerate and rise again. However the beast is banished, it is important to salt and burn the remains and scatter the ashes lest they rise and seek revenge.

LIFECYCLE: 101 days under the curse, or a lifetime, until cured, killed, or passed on.

HISTORY: Accounts of Rougarou go all the way back to medieval France.

Through the 1600s, the condition was believed to be hereditary, with the one afflicted leading a normal life, unsuspecting until something triggered the transformation changing their physique and leaving them with a hunger for raw meat. The change was not complete unless they took a bite of human flesh.

One of the most notable cases, from France in the late

1700s, tells of one that has come to be known as the Beast of Gévaudan. This Rougarou terrorized the region for three years, said to have slaughtered between sixty and one hundred people before being put down by three bullets made from a melted-down silver baptismal chalice that had been blessed.

Some accounts, however, have no basis in French culture. In the Louisiana region of the early 1700s, the Attakapa were at war with the Opelousas and the Chitimacha tribes. This native tribe was known for its blood-thirsty nature and for consuming human flesh. When they lost their war, the few survivors fled into the swamp, where it is said they encountered an evil spirit that possessed them, granting them the power to shapeshift. Legend says that the Attakapa embraced their bestial nature and cravings for human flesh and blood, becoming the Wolf-Walkers terrorizing the region.

Southern Louisiana, the territory of the Rougarou, has been plagued by animal mutilations and strange, violent deaths as recently as the mid-to-late 2010s. Some accounts have reached as far as Texas, Colorado, and Alabama.

About the Artist

Although Jason Whitley has worn many creative hats, he is at heart a traditional illustrator and painter. With author James Chambers, Jason collaborates and illustrates the sometimes-prose, sometimes graphic novel, *The Midnight Hour,* which is being collected into one volume by eSpec Books. His and Scott Eckelaert's newspaper comic strip, Sea Urchins, has been collected into four volumes. Along with eSpec Books' Systema Paradoxa series, Jason is working on a crime noir graphic novel. His portrait of Charlotte Hawkins Brown is on display in the Charlotte Hawkins Brown Museum.

CAPTURE THE CRYPTIDS!

Cryptid Crate is a monthly subscription box filled with various cryptozoology and paranormal themed items to wear, display and collect. Expect a carefully curated box filled with creeptastic pieces from indie makers and artisans pertaining to bigfoot, sasquatch, UFOs, ghosts, and other cryptid and mysterious creatures (apparel, decor, media, etc).

http://CryptidCrate.com